CHRISTMAS KNIGHT
A KNIGHTS THROUGH TIME TRAVEL ROMANCE

CYNTHIA LUHRS

D1521113

Copyright © 2022 by Cynthia Luhrs

All rights reserved.

No part of this book may be reproduced in any form or by any electronic or mechanical means, including information storage and retrieval systems, without written permission from the author, except for the use of brief quotations in a book review.

P resent Day
    London, England
    December

J ANE R ANDALL WOULD NEVER FORGET THE FIRST TIME SHE laid eyes on Josie Simmons, the biggest star in Hollywood. Nor would she ever forget what happened that summer morning.

The movie star was even more beautiful in person, California sunshine caressed her golden skin, she had a flawless complexion, big green eyes, and a body that made grown men weep and women green with envy.

When a painfully shy teenage girl approached, instead of turning her away as she came out of the shop, Josie stopped, smiled and turned her full attention on the girl, as if nothing else in the world mattered. That one small act had quelled her doubts. Jane started working for Josie that very day.

Too bad it was all an act. The few stories she'd been able to dig up were true, though if she'd known how awful her boss was, then Jane wouldn't be here today. London, England, was a very long way from her home in California.

The skies were the same dirty gray as the buildings as rain drizzled down, and everywhere she looked, black umbrellas dotted the streets. The locals went about their day while Jane shivered in her new black quilted vest, just like Martha Stewart.

She peered out from underneath the red umbrella and decided it could rain the entire time and it wouldn't matter. Before she left, her mom asked Jane to promise she'd try to have fun. To move on with her life. A small snort escaped. Her mom was a fine one to talk, holding onto the surf shop, refusing to date even though it had been over a year. But a promise was a promise, so Jane would try.

There wasn't a porter to be found to help with the luggage, not with a big security convention in town and all the tourists coming and going. By the time Jane collected the mountain of baggage, wheeled it to the car for the driver to load, then ran back inside the terminal to meet her boss, the hottest star in Hollywood, she was sweating and swaying on her feet with exhaustion.

"Jane. Jane, are you listening?"

The high-pitched voice sliced through the fog rolling through her brain, making her wince.

She blinked, turned to face her boss, stumbled over an

errant Hermes bag Josie had casually dropped on the dirty floor, and went sprawling.

"Get up. You're embarrassing me," Josie hissed, tapping one booted foot.

"I'm fine."

Jane scrambled to her feet, dusting herself off, gritting her teeth at the pain in her shoulder.

"I've seen to the luggage. The driver is waiting, so whenever you're ready, we can go. The hotel is on standby for your arrival."

Josie glanced up from the crystal-encrusted phone, scowling, as she waved a perfectly manicured hand in the air.

"Can't you do something with that enormous mess of hair?"

She frowned, which surprised Jane, as most of the Hollywood stars she'd been exposed to used so much Botox and fillers that they had a hard time with expressions, but not Josie. She knew she needed her face to move to convey emotion on-screen. Everyone said her doctor was the best in the world, with a light touch that took years off, but left the ability to move one's face.

The imperious tone penetrated the exhaustion as Josie looked Jane up and down, finding her lacking.

"I'll give you a bonus if you chop it off tonight."

In her humble opinion, Jane had always thought her hair was her best feature. It was a mix of shades from caramel brown to honey blond, thick and wavy, requiring nothing more than washing and letting it air dry for it to look good. Hair colorists drooled over the colors and perfect wavy curls while random strangers stopped her in the street, at stores, and in the airport, all wanting to know who did her hair.

Instead of saying what was on the tip of her tongue, Jane quickly wound her hair up into a messy bun, tying a scarf around it to contain the thick bun. Hair elastics, even the large ones wouldn't fit around her ponytail. She'd finally found someone who made extra-large elastics and ordered a boxful. Usually she had several in a pocket or on her wrist, but she'd taken them off before boarding the flight and hadn't had time to dig through her tote bag to find one.

They made their way through the terminal, out into overcast skies and drizzle, security keeping several overzealous fans and photographers away from her boss as Josie complained the entire time under her breath about how awful the weather was and how was she supposed to look her best when the wind kept blowing?

How she could smile and wave as people stopped and stared, taking pictures of her, yet still complain about every single little thing was a skill Jane envied.

The private jet had been unavailable, undergoing overdue maintenance. Rock stars performing at a festival for the bombing victims in Spain had already booked most of the charters. The studio loaned their jet to Josie's co-star to fly to Australia, causing Josie to fly commercial from California to Heathrow.

Josie flew first class, which in her boss's opinion was on the same level as being strapped on top of a rickety bus in India crammed full of people, livestock, and smelly food. Not that her boss had ever subjected herself to such conditions, but she knew what that would be like, she'd informed Jane in a matter-of-fact tone of voice.

As they had arranged the flight last-minute, Jane found herself crammed into economy, which wasn't unusual as Josie always made her sit in coach if they had to lower themselves to fly commercial.

No, it was being stuck for the full duration of an international flight in the middle seat between a man who obviously ate steroids for breakfast, lunch, and dinner, judging by the size of his arms and legs, which kept taking up valuable real estate. While on the other side of her, was a woman who wore enough perfume to keep the perfumeries of Paris in business for the next ten years.

As an added bonus, the smelly woman was sobbing over a breakup and coughing all over Jane as the woman apologized, saying it wasn't the plague, just an awful cold. Jane hoped the woman was being honest and that it wasn't something worse. It was a most uncomfortable, exhausting flight, leaving Jane stuffed up, achy, and worn out.

When they arrived at the airport, they found that all the private cars were already booked for some big security convention. Josie stomped her tiny foot from the comfort of the private airline lounge as Jane scrambled to find suitable transportation.

She'd stalked the rental area and when a man came striding across the lobby, whistling to himself, keys in hand, she followed him and booked what had to have been the last private car in all of London. Thank goodness it was black with tinted windows, as no other color was acceptable.

Then Jane took care of the luggage and went to fetch her boss while the driver assured her the car was clean and he'd restock the water Josie liked, then he'd meet her out front. He left, whistling to himself, unaware of heads turning as he passed by. The guy looked like a young Tom Cruise.

Upon noticing the car, the driver waiting patiently with the door open, Josie stopped, pulled huge black oversized sunglasses down her nose, looked over the frames and arched one famous brow.

It didn't matter the day was overcast and rainy. Her boss always wore sunglasses when she went out.

"What is *that?*"

Josie pointed at the car, tapping her booted foot. When Jane didn't answer right away, the tapping intensified.

Was she missing something? Mentally, Jane went through the checklist in her head.

"It's our ride. Black car, black tinted windows."

The car looked fine to her, though the guy was dressed in a black suit rather than a uniform. Maybe that was it?

Josie huffed out a breath, baring perfectly blinding white teeth as Jane swallowed, unconsciously taking three steps back.

"It isn't shiny enough."

It was going to be one of *those* trips.

Last week Josie threw a tantrum when the car that picked her up at the estate she was renting wasn't shiny enough. She threw her water bottle at Jane, barely missing her head.

When Jane logically asked how the car was supposed to be shiny when it was pouring down rain, Josie threw her phone.

Thanks to quick reflexes, Jane ducked. The phone went sailing end over end and landed in the duck pond with a splash. Shortly thereafter Jane found herself wading through the moss green smelly pond for almost three hours, looking for the sparkly phone as a raft of ducks happily paddled alongside her, quacking as if to say, *what are you doing in here with us?*

Perhaps it would have been better to let the phone hit her smack in the face.

Note to self. Abscond with a suit of armor from the castle where they were filming, then spoiled Josie could throw as many phones as she liked.

Why hadn't anyone told her the truth about working for Josie? The studio must have some serious hackers or cash on hand to have kept so many stories of how terribly she treated her assistants out of the press.

There wasn't one single negative story about working for her. Oh sure, there were the usual stories about being a diva, but Jane thought all big stars had to be a little spoiled.

How wrong she'd been. After her first week, she found out from other assistants how terrible her boss was to anyone who worked for her, especially attractive women. Considering herself average, Jane thought she was in the clear, but she'd heard through the grapevine that Josie had called her stunning and was jealous of Jane's hair. Thanks to hair extensions, no one knew how thin Josie's hair was, not even the men she dated. Jane only knew because all the assistants kept a group text going where they warned and updated each other on their bosses or who might be looking for a new assistant.

On the bright side, they all agreed if she survived working

for Josie, she'd have her pick of jobs in the industry. Though after being on set and around Josie, Jane didn't want to work in Hollywood. Then again, she didn't really know what she wanted to do with her life.

Her mom had defied her wealthy parents, skipped college and learned how to be a make-up artist. Then she met Jane's dad, a professional surfer. They fell madly in love. Her mom moved to the beach, and they opened a surf shop, then had Jane a year later. Their biggest disappointment.

Awful Josie flounced the three steps to the car, haranguing Jane during the entire ride from the airport to the hotel as Jane looked out the window, up at the gray skies and wondered if they might have a white Christmas? For as long as she could remember, she'd always wanted to see snow, something she'd never had growing up at the beach in sunny California.

The car smelled funny. They didn't have the right bottled water. The windows were too dark. The car was too noisy. And why wasn't the sun shining?

Her boss went on and on, the complaints never-ending as the driver sped up, eager to get them to their destination and escape as fast as he could.

Working for Josie was utterly exhausting. As the car pulled up to the hotel, Josie reached across Jane, hand on the door handle so she couldn't get out, while the driver stood outside waiting for directions.

"No more mistakes. I did Regina a huge favor by hiring you. Don't make me regret it."

Regina was a friend of Jane's mother. She was married to

some Hollywood bigwig and had known Melinda since prep school.

Not bothering to wait for a response, Josie exited the vehicle, smile firmly in place, waving to the paparazzi she'd had Jane call on the way from the airport, as she swept into the hotel, leaving her to deal with the luggage and checking them in while Josie posed for pictures and signed autographs for fans.

The relationship between celebrities and the press had changed a great deal over the years. It wasn't the awful hounding like when Britney Spears had her breakdown for the entire world to see, and during the era of the late Princess Diana.

Now? Celebs worked with the press, calling them to make sure they photographed them, then faking outrage and annoyance at always being followed and photographed, never getting any privacy. Many of them were so controlling of their image that they required approval on all photos before allowing them to go to print.

A certain family, infamous for the extreme editing of their images to ensure they looked a certain way, was notorious for how they controlled their social media presence. The funny thing was, they didn't even look like real women in the photos.

When Jane met them on a private island where Josie was vacationing, she didn't even recognize the women in person. Beauty ideals had become so distorted that Jane was convinced that seeing a picture of an ordinary, unadulterated pretty woman on social media would soon become a novelty.

The press played along, knowing if they developed a good working relationship, their publication, or they, as freelancers, would get first dibs on the best photo opportunities.

Some celebrities, along with reality stars and influencers, were so desperate to stay in the public eye they'd even call the press for what they called private moments. Jane always snorted hearing that. If it was a private moment, why call the press? Just do the good deed and move on like Keanu Reeves. But nope, this was the hungry machine of social media and it demanded to be fed regularly or the influencer, reality star, disgraced royals, or other celebrity risked losing the attention of the public as they moved on to the next scandal. The public was just as fickle as the stars.

Okay, fine. Jane could admit it. She had become a cynic since working in Hollywood. Everything seemed to be fake. So much so, she longed for someone real. A genuine conversation without the guy looking around the room for someone more important. Was it too much to ask for a guy to be interested in what she thought, not who she knew or what she could do for him?

Jane met Josie in her suite, careful not to knock over any of the flower arrangements that had been delivered. It smelled like a florist shop, exactly the way her boss liked.

Once she tipped the bellman, unpacked all of Josie's clothes, and made sure they delivered the right bottled water, wine, and fresh fruit. Jane made her way from the bedroom out to the living area. She waited, looking out the floor-to-ceiling windows at the iconic sights of London while Josie lounged on a huge white sofa, scrolling through her phone.

When she finally looked up, the most wanted woman in Hollywood let out a dramatic sigh.

"Honestly, you are going to have to make more of an effort."

She waved a hand up and down in front of Jane.

"You are a rumpled mess. Why didn't you change before we landed? It's bad enough I have a chunky assistant who is average looking at best, but honestly? Can't you try? Don't you care?"

She pursed her lips, a look of distaste on her face.

Jane dressed in embroidered jeans, a white long-sleeved tee shirt, a gray cashmere sweater, and short boots. Over it, she wore the black puffy vest. She thought she looked fine. Guess not.

"You look sick. Put on some makeup."

Then she cringed, dramatically clapping her hands over her mouth and nose, eyes huge.

"You're not sick, are you? I cannot get sick."

Hastily, before Josie could throw one of her infamous tantrums, Jane reassured her.

"I'm fine. Just tired. I'll put on some makeup after I unpack."

Jane knew she was average looking, but there was nothing wrong with average. And okay, sure, she could stand to lose ten pounds. By regular standards, she was fine, but this was Hollywood and by their standards, she was overweight. The thought of going on a diet to appease her boss made Jane crave pizza and ice cream.

Startled, Josie sat up, the phone sliding off her thighs to land on the plush carpet.

"Go find that tea I like. You know I have to have my tea this afternoon. I'm going to take a nap so I don't get rundown from whatever germs you're breathing on me."

Without waiting for an answer, Josie scooped up her phone and glided to the bedroom, perfume competing with the flowers.

Careful not to let the door make any noise when it closed, Jane leaned against the wall for a moment before looking at her room key, then stuffing it in the pocket of her jeans.

Jet-lagged, muscles aching from contorting herself into the middle seat on the plane and then tripping over the bags at the airport, Jane wanted nothing more than to climb into bed and sleep until the next morning.

Instead, she went downstairs and out into the chilly day, grateful for the warm scarf one of her mom's friends had knitted for her as a birthday gift. It was thick and cozy; the yarn variegated in shades of purple and blue. It might be fifty-three today, but it was rainy, which made it feel colder, and she was from the land of sunshine so she was always cold.

London was beautiful. The rain turned the streets and buildings into a historical TV show. When they traveled, Jane was so busy she rarely had time to sightsee. Usually she would take public transportation or a cab, but since Josie was sleeping, she took the private car so she could get back before her boss woke and terrorized the staff.

"Where to, miss?"

The driver looked relieved it was only her.

She smiled as she climbed into the warm interior.

"I have to find a certain kind of tea."

He grinned as he climbed into the car.

"There are plenty of tea shops. We'll take the scenic route."

There was so much to take in. Jane's eyes were gritty by the third stop.

They visited seven shops before she found the exact brand and flavor of tea Josie preferred. Normally, Jane would have packed it or called ahead to have it waiting in the room, but the other assistant was supposed to have taken care of it.

Josie liked to have two assistants at all times, though in the five months, six days, and nine hours that Jane had worked for her, no one had lasted longer than a week or two. The last second assistant only lasted half a day before he fled, sobbing. That was why they all had to sign agreements stating they would not talk about their time working for Josie.

Thank goodness, she only had one month, three weeks, four days, and fifteen hours until she was free. No more demands for a different pillow at two-thirty in the morning.

No more ridiculous errands such as fetching a pair of shoes from a house in another country, and then upon returning on a redeye flight where she was squashed in the center seat in coach, her spoiled boss decided she didn't want those shoes after all, and sent Jane to go find a pair of shoes she saw in a fashion show by some designer who she couldn't remember his name.

What had she been thinking to take a job as a personal assistant to the most spoiled movie star in all of Hollywood?

Oh, right. The promise to her mom. Her mom swore it would be fun, that boring Jane could go to parties, kiss boys, get a little drunk and lose her shoes. She knew it disappointed her parents that she wasn't as free-spirited as they were.

Her mom's parents left her mom a small inheritance, the rest went to Jane. She couldn't access the trust until she was twenty-five.

The money she earned on this job would be enough to allow her to spend a year in England in a tiny cottage at the edge of a forest.

Jane met a woman on the set of a film where Josie had a cameo, playing herself. The woman was a master gardener and showed Jane pictures of all the cottage gardens she'd created. She told Jane stories about old forests and magic.

After that, Jane searched and searched until she found a picture perfect cottage. And if deep in the forest, the snow kept her in until spring, it would be fine. Sure, she knew it would only be a couple of inches if that, but to her, any snow would be amazing.

She was looking forward to watching the snow fall while she sat in front of a fire, wrapped in a quilt, drinking hot cocoa, and trying to figure out what to do with her life. Sure, she could live off the trust fund and do nothing, but she wanted to have a purpose.

As of January thirty-first, this difficult period in her life would be over and Jane would once again be free to do as she pleased. To wake when she wished, go where she wanted, and to turn off her phone whenever the whim struck.

Maybe she'd even get rid of her phone for the year altogether and go back to mailing actual letters... a girl could dream.

The phone she kept for Josie had been ringing and pinging with texts the entire time so that she had to make several additional stops before arriving back at the hotel.

By the time she delivered the tea, withstood Josie yelling at her about the car that would take her to and from the set, how the sheets on the bed were scratchy, the pillows weren't plump enough, and there weren't nearly enough flowers in the room. If there had been one more bouquet, Jane would have lost her boss within the blooms.

By the time Jane staggered to the small but pretty room, she yanked the comforter off and flopped face down on the bed, inhaling the faint scent of lavender. Given how Josie liked to call at all hours of the day and night, she'd better sleep while she could.

As if thinking of the devil incarnate conjured her, thirteen texts dinged on the phone, one after another. It seemed Jane was immediately required. Something about a hair emergency.

A sound that was a mixture of a groan and a sob escaped as she scrubbed her hands over her face. It seemed Josie needed a special treatment for her hair.

"Think of the cottage. Get through the next month, three weeks, four days, and three hours, and you can sleep as long as you want."

With a yawn, she stretched, splashed water on her face, and staggered out to the waiting car. The driver gave her a look she'd quickly come to recognize during her time working for her boss. It was a mixture of pity, annoyance, and a bit of awe that Jane could deal with the diva.

"I'm making double pay for this gig. Hope you are, love."

"Not a chance."

With a tired smile, Jane looked up at the silver sky, wishing she could disappear to a place without phones or movie stars.

Once inside the sleek black sedan, she rested her chin in her hand as she watched the scenery from behind yet another piece of glass.

$\mathfrak{R}$ 2 $\mathfrak{R}$

348—England
Winter

I NICHOLAS MONTGOMERY STOMPED OUT OF HIS SIRE'S HALL, grumbling under his breath, sword banging against his hip, as he made his way to the lists to vent his frustration on the garrison.

Yet another excuse as to why his intended had not yet arrived at Winterborne Keep. When Nicholas snarled at the messenger, his sire assured him the gel would set sail in a se'n-night and when she arrived, after they were sure none were ill, they would make haste to the chapel so he could finally wed. Two long years he had waited to take her to wife.

Then his sire, Gavin, Lord of Greystone Castle, clapped

him on the back, telling Nicholas to enjoy his freedom whilst it lasted. Though this last bit was said with a look over his shoulder to make sure Lady Greystone was not present.

Nicholas kicked at the dust, swearing under his breath though not quietly enough for one of his father's guard chuckled.

"You. You shall go first."

Nicholas narrowed his eyes at the man, gratified when the knight let out a squeak.

The captain of his own guard appeared silently by his side.

"The gel will present herself before the year is over. Her sire is known for having the fastest ships in the land."

He glanced at the sky.

"The weather will hold, the ships will sail swiftly. They will not be ill. Then you will wed, have babes and be eager for war so you may leave her and her shrewish tongue behind at Winterborne."

Nicholas clapped the most fierce knight in his personal guard on the shoulder.

"Mayhap she will be a biddable lass, quiet and meek."

A snort was the only answer he received.

Aye, they would wed and settle into day-to-day life, his wife seeing to the household and the babes. Then once he produced an heir and a spare, Nicholas would busy himself hunting, seeing to his estates, and in time he would ride off to war, for there was always another war. Though of late, there had been rumblings of a distant illness spreading across the lands. The king's own daughter had perished of the Great Pestilence. The priests said 'twas a punishment from God though Hugh, his middle brother who was a monk, said the illness came from distant lands carried to England by ship.

Perchance, in time, Nicholas and his intended would grow to care for one another. He was not so childish as to believe in a love match. Most nobility married for title, gold, and lands. 'Twas a rare occurrence for a couple to wed for love, as his parents had done.

Even though his mother, Mary, brought an enormous dowry with her, his sire swore he had fallen in love with her the moment he spied her shooting an arrow at a target from horseback.

With a snort, he pushed thoughts of love and marriage aside as he worked his way through his men and his father's garrison, but 'twas not enough. His sire said perhaps Nicholas might wish to wed a woman he could converse with, much like his own mother?

Nay, he wanted no opinionated lass, but a quiet lass who knew her place and left him in peace.

The men were panting and leaning on their swords by the time he ran through them a third time, so Nicholas sent them on their way as he leaned against the stone wall, one booted foot crossed, contemplating his intended.

A woman equal to him, able to discuss matters, one always by his side... mayhap that would be better than a quiet, bidd-able wife like his brother Alfred wed. She usually shrieked and fled at the sight of him, making Nicholas wonder how they had produced a babe, when she ran from the room whenever Alfred appeared. She was beautiful, if bland.

Hrumph. Had he been wrong all these years? A long-suffering sigh escaped as Nicholas pushed off from the wall. There was plenty of time to think on what kind of wife he wanted. Someone to talk to by the fire at night about their respective days... 'twas a most pleasant thought, if one not shared by most nobles.

❦

By the time Nicholas and the men arrived at Winterborne, a fortnight had passed. Whilst he was gone, a messenger arrived with a parcel. In it was a miniature portrait of his intended, along with a letter informing him she would arrive three weeks hence. Her hair was covered, so he could not tell the color. A modest face peered out at him with pale skin, light eyes, and a pleasing countenance.

Hugh took the oval from him, frowning as he squinted at the portrait.

"See the small smile? She is laughing at you, likely knowing her sire paid the painter handsomely to ensure a most pleasing portrait. 'Tis a common deception."

His brother handed the miniature back with a grin.

"In truth, this one might look like your horse or old Agnes, the washerwoman, with only half her teeth and a hump on her back."

Startled by the thought, Nicholas almost dropped the portrait. "Nay, he would not portray his daughter as beautiful if she were not."

He ran a hand through his hair until it was standing up.

"Would he?"

Hugh clapped him on the shoulder.

"We shall know soon enough. When she stands next to you at the altar, make sure you look under the veil to make sure she is as shown before you pledge your troth to her."

Hugh strode through the muck, robes dragging as they made their way back to the relative comfort of the hall. At least the roof no longer leaked, so his betrothed would not have rain coming down on her head, nor birds roosting above the high table.

His sire gifted Nicholas Winterborne as a betrothal gift, leaving out the fact that the place needed enough repairs to deplete the funds Nicholas had earned warring across the continent. Especially as the summer had been unnaturally wet. The grain lay rotting in the fields. With such a poor harvest, there were already food shortages, though fortunately not at Greystone and now not at Winterborne, thanks to his mother.

She sent several servants along with furniture and food to stock the larder so he would have a place to sleep, a full belly, and a chair to sit by the fire. The cellar was full of wine. It was the first thing he had seen to when he arrived.

Hugh clasped his shoulder.

"If you do not wish me to wed the two of you, we will send the gel back to her father." He paused. "I have heard the pestilence has already swept across the lands. It might not be safe for her. Mayhap she could stay in a convent until 'tis over."

Instead of answering, Nicholas took the stairs to the underground passage that led from the larder to the main well beneath the courtyard, which supplied the keep with water. He pulled up a bucket and dipped a ladle into the cold, sweet water. When he held the ladle out to Hugh, his brother grimaced.

"I would prefer a cup of ale."

They stopped in the kitchens, the scent of baking bread making his stomach rumble. The ovens were set into arches in the wall; the kitchen was in a separate tower. With three enormous hearths constantly in use, the kitchens were the best place to linger in the winter when 'twas cold and gloomy outside.

"My lord." The boy helping the cook handed him a cup of warm spiced wine then fetched a cup of ale for Hugh.

He nodded his thanks as he sat at the end of a long scarred wooden table that likely had seen its share of battles and other less savory things in the years it had stood watch in the kitchens.

They stretched their feet towards the fire, out of the way while the servants went about their business.

Hugh looked around the tower.

"Winterborne is a fine, solid home. Do not worry about the gel or what may come. We die when 'tis our time. Fill the castle with sons and live a long life."

Nicholas searched his brother's face.

"You are not given to such thoughts. Is aught amiss?"

He had always wondered...

"Did ye always wish to be a monk?"

Hugh drained the cup and stood.

"Come, let us walk. I find myself filled with worrisome thoughts of late."

Content to wait for his brother to tell him what was bothering him, Nicholas tried to look at the castle through the eyes of his soon-to-be bride.

His solar and the other chambers facing the inner courtyard had glazed windows with a greenish thick glass full of ripples and bubbles. One had to open them to look outside. This time of year, the shutters were usually closed to help keep out the cold.

The ceiling in the great hall was thirty feet high and twice as long, with clean rushes on the floor. He had three tapestries safely packed away to hang on the walls, which had been freshly whitewashed.

They passed through the hall, outside, through the courtyard, passed the fallow gardens, and made their way to the battlements.

They had built Winterborne to keep out the Welsh. There were murder holes, trip steps, arrow slits, and heavy barred doors on every chamber.

The portcullis boasted wicked-looking spikes, and the battlements which were at least sixty feet high looked out over the glorious countryside as the land rested for winter. When he turned around, he could see the Channel, smell the clean salty air, which helped keep the cesspit odors at bay.

"Have you heard the rumors?"

Hugh leaned against the wall as Nicholas looked down at the moat that encircled the keep. 'Twas deep with sharp wooden spikes at the bottom, waiting to impale his enemies.

The lands were rich, full of game with good soil for farming, and the sea for fishing.

He turned away from his lands to meet his brother's troubled gaze.

"Aye. Have more ships arrived with dead sailors?"

Nicholas pursed his lips.

"'Tis spreading across the lands, killing many."

"We are no longer welcoming travelers to the abbey. The summer was wet, grain rotted in the fields. You know 'twill be a hard winter. You must take care, brother. Do not let any travelers pass through the gates if they are fevered or have black spots."

"Black spots?"

Hugh shook his head.

"One of the monks said 'tis awful. People have fever, vomiting, and cough up blood. They have black sores on the skin and die in three days. We must be wary."

Then he blinked and turned to look out over the land.

"Winter always makes me melancholy. Few travelers come to Winterborne. You should be safe. Now, tell me about your new floors."

He grinned at Nicholas.

"I did not think you would have rushes covering them, as they were all Alfred could talk about when he visited the abbey. I hear he is having his chamber floor laid with new tile."

"I thank ye for sending the laborers here."

His brother had sent them to Winterborne after the men had finished a room for high-ranking visitors at the abbey.

They created the patterns on the tiles with different colored clay. Some had two colors, while others had six different colors. 'Twas a marvel. Though best not to think about the cost or Nicholas would faint like the minstrel his mother had sent, who swooned whenever he had a fright.

He contented himself knowing that the pattern of the tiles was not just on the surface but all the way through the clay, and as the tiles wore down they would still be beautiful.

There were leaves, flowers, animals and various shapes that made up the patterns on the floors of the great hall, solar, and one chamber for guests.

The workers crafted the tiles last spring and summer when it was dry. The men finished early, thankfully, as the latter part of summer had been particularly wet this year.

The clay was dug in the winter and left to weather until needed in the spring. There was a kiln near to Winterborne at an estate owned by Edward who rarely visited, as it was one of his many properties.

Nicholas and the other nobles had gone to see how the tiles were crafted after seeing the ornate floor at the abbey.

They made their way down from the battlements to the stables, the horses warm and happily munching hay.

He was glad the abbey had given Hugh leave to see him settled at Winterborne. Then again, his father gave generously to the abbey and they would want to continue to receive his gold.

He had left the keep in the care of a steward, a cousin named Alan. When they arrived and Nicholas saw the disrepair, he almost took his cousin's head as the man stood wringing his hands, excuses falling from his blubbering lips.

The newly installed glorious tile floors were hidden under layers of muck and grime. Dogs fought over bones on the floor as Nicholas cursed in five languages. Most of the keep had stone floors as 'twas outrageously expensive to have the tiles made.

Hugh clapped him on the shoulder and sent Alan and his servants back to his sire. Then he'd told Nicholas not to worry, for they had food, drink, and servants to see to the mess.

The garrison, stables, smithy and other outbuildings were in various states of ruin.

When his mother found out, she sent an army of servants to scour the keep from top to bottom, builders to fix the hole in the roof and the outbuildings, and food for his larder along with furniture. If she had been born a man, Nicholas knew she would have commanded great armies.

3

The next week passed in a blur. Between traveling to the set at the castle and running errands for Josie, Jane was worn out.

Thanks to the driver knowing the fastest ways around the city, she'd sneaked in a quick trip to the Tower of London and a couple of museums, but mostly it was various high end shops, where a tiny bottle of hand soap cost fifty dollars. Fifty dollars? Not to mention, Josie would leave the partial bottles behind when she left, so Jane always took them with her, not wanting to waste the outrageously priced hand soap.

Jane liked the watermelon or grapefruit hand soap from Walmart or Target that she could get for around a dollar a bottle. Guess that was the difference between a regular person and a rich movie star.

Don't get her started on foaming hand soap. One of her friends used to say she splurged and bought rich people soap.

Sure the foam was creamy and nice but the soap never lasted as long as regular soap in a pump.

Jane's parents had plenty of money but they weren't frivolous, instead preferring to spend money on experiences, like going to Fiji to dive, or to Italy for a festival. Before she'd left for London, Jane had begged her mom to go to Bermuda. Her friends had been asking and her mom hadn't taken a trip since her dad died.

It rained steadily all morning, lending an authentic air to the shoot, when Josie summoned her to the trailer.

The air inside smelled of eucalyptus, lavender, and sandalwood. Jane waved the humid, foggy air aside as she made her way through the trailer, stopping in the kitchenette to pour a cup of tea.

"Josie?"

"Back here." The muffled voice croaked.

Her boss sprawled out on the sofa, wrapped in a blanket, nose red, eyes glassy.

Knowing better than to tell Josie she looked awful, Jane handed her a mug of hot tea, liberally laced with honey and a splash of bourbon.

"Thank you."

Wow, Josie must be feeling lousy. It was rare for her to thank anyone, unless she was in the public eye. Like the time she'd gone to serve food at a homeless shelter, a private moment. Right. So private, the press just happened to be walking by when Josie went in? Nope. Jane knew for a fact someone had alerted them to the photo op, because she'd made the call on behalf of her boss.

"I have a scene tomorrow afternoon that can't be delayed. You must go to Bath. I need the healing waters to steam my face and get rid of this dreadful cold."

She touched her nose and winced.

"Look at me. I look like Rudolph, ready to guide the sleigh at Christmas."

Knowing better than to say anything about how Josie looked, Jane nodded.

"I'll go straightaway."

Josie sneezed. "Take the car, I'm not going anywhere in this dreadful weather. Why does it have to rain so much?"

Her boss took another sip of tea and closed her eyes.

Did it matter that you could no longer take the waters in Bath because of the water quality?

Nope. Not to Josie. The first assistant called as Jane made her way through the castle grounds to the waiting car. The castle was small. They'd built it in the seventeen hundreds based on how some lord thought a keep should look. It wasn't nearly as forbidding as one of those imposing medieval fortresses dotting the countryside with their gray stone, damp walls, and rats in the cellars. Not that Jane cared who built it or when. While she knew it was important to remember history, she certainly didn't want to live it every day.

Give her hot showers, central heat and air, ice whenever she wanted it, and a microwave any day.

Bill cleared his throat.

"Jane? Did you get all that?"

She made the notes in her phone then took him off speaker.

"Got it. Three gallons of water from Bath. Wouldn't it be a lot easier to go to the nearby Thermae Bath Spa for the water?"

The natural thermal waters fed the spa, and they made sure there weren't any brain-eating bacteria in the water.

Bill laughed, a high-pitched, slightly unhinged laugh.

"You do not know what I've had to go through to make this happen. Josie wants the water from the source. She swears the treated water the spa uses isn't good enough to magically cure her cold."

"Sounds like Josie."

He muttered something under his breath before adding, "I'm supposed to be off for two days at Christmas. I'll email you with anything that needs to be taken care of. You know how Josie gets around the holidays when she isn't seeing anyone. It isn't pretty."

Oh, she knew alright. Over the Fourth of July, Josie had sulked, gotten drunk, and then slept with an actor with a terrible reputation for falling in love with his leading lady and then dumping her when the shoot ended. They were shooting a couple of commercials for an obscene amount of money and that was exactly what had happened. The rest of the summer had been miserable until Josie started this new movie.

Jane was glad Bill had arranged everything so all she had to do was pick up the jugs of water. Otherwise, she might have been tempted to fill the jugs from the spigot. She frowned. No, she was too honest for her own good to do such a thing, no matter how tempting. Plastering a bright smile on her face, she waved at the driver.

"Here we go again."

He grinned and handed her a to go cup of hot chocolate with loads of whipped cream.

"Thank you. I missed lunch. If you weren't married, I'd propose."

"I know a bloke who'd happily bring you all the hot cocoa you want. Say the word and I'll set you up."

Settled into the plush, warm car, Jane leaned her head against the seat, hoping she wasn't coming down with Josie's cold.

"While I appreciate the thought, I don't have any time to date, not with how much Josie has me running."

She let out a breath.

"Someday. Someday when I have a cottage in the woods, then I'll call you and let you play matchmaker."

They were still in London when the driver pulled over on a side street, parked, and lowered the privacy window.

"My mum's been in a car accident."

His voice shook.

"It's bad. I'm sorry I can't take you. The agency will send another driver. I'll wait here until they do."

Jane leaned over the seat.

"I'm so sorry. I hope she'll be okay."

She gathered up her small backpack, grabbed two bottles of water along with a bag of nuts and opened the car door.

"Wait." He jumped out of the car.

She shook her head. "Go. Family comes first. I'll take a bus or something."

He scrubbed a hand over his face. "Get in. The bus station is on the way to the hospital. I'll drop you."

"You don't need to do that."

"Get in the car, we're wasting time."

Grateful she didn't have to find a bus station, Josie jumped back in the car.

His hand shook as he closed the door. They sped through London traffic, and for once, Jane did not look out the window. Going fast through traffic always made her nervous, so instead she looked up the bus information, noted the trip would take a little over three hours each way. Plenty of time.

When he skidded to a stop, she jumped out, leaning down next to his window.

"Thank you. I hope your mum's okay."

He was gone before she made it through the front doors. The bus was leaving in ten minutes, plenty of time for a bathroom break and to grab a bit of sustenance. Who knew if she'd have time to eat later? No way was she missing dinner as well.

Jane sat on a bench and went through her pink leather backpack. There were several packs of hand warmers, not that she'd need them, but when she'd left California for England, she had no idea how cold she'd feel. In her whole life, the only time she'd ever seen snow was in a movie.

There were chargers for her phone and tablet, notepad and pen, two candy bars, wallet, and trusty container of lip balm. The bag of nuts, both bottles of water, and a few other road trip snacks went into the pretty backpack.

She tied her hair back with a scarf and made her way to

the bus. On the way, she called the car company who assured her they would have a car pick her up in Bath to bring her back. They gave her the name of a florist so she could have flowers delivered to the hospital.

Josie must have taken cold medicine since she hadn't called or texted since Jane left. The drugs always knocked her boss out for a good eight hours.

Dressed in a pair of leggings, comfortable low boots, a long-sleeved tee and a cozy sweater, she was plenty warm.

A combination of the low hum of the wheels, the voices of the other passengers, and general exhaustion lulled Jane to sleep, her scarf tucked between her head and the chilly window.

The sound of music woke her. She stretched to work out the kinks in her shoulder before checking the time. One more hour to go.

Celebrities were not normal. Was it because they'd gotten so used to no one telling them no, catering to their every whim, and doing nothing for themselves? Or had they always been difficult and becoming a star had made it worse?

When her mom had talked the job up, words like fun, glamorous, and exciting, were tossed around. She'd told Jane she needed to get away, get her mind off what had happened. Leave the ocean behind for a bit, and for once act like a crazy twenty-something.

Thoughts of slipping into dusty antique shops, bookshops, and old buildings on her promised two days off a week cemented the deal.

What a load of nonsense. Not only did Jane not get the

promised two days off a week, she was on call twenty-four hours a day, seven days a week, and had yet to see a single penny of overtime. Not to mention her boss had skipped Thanksgiving, saying she didn't want to eat carbs so Jane contented herself with a to go turkey dinner in between running errands.

The job was supposed to be easy, the star a dream to work for. A snort escaped as the bus bumped over a rut in the road. Josie Simmons had to be the biggest spoiled brat in the world. Jane had to hand it to her public relations people, they'd kept the star's outrageous and mean behavior out of the public eye, a laborious task in the age of social media.

By the time they arrived, Jane was glad to stretch her legs, and delighted to see the famous Christmas market in full swing. People were bustling around, shopping at the various vendors, Christmas carolers lent a festive air to the market, and there were several street performers. Overlaid on top of everything was the mineral scent from the waters carried on the air.

The car wouldn't arrive for a couple of hours, plenty of time to meet the man with the miracle water and to tour the baths.

Jane meandered along, wandering the crescents and square, feeling like she was on a film set, which given how many had been filmed here, wasn't surprising. The architecture was stunning, the honey-colored stone beautiful.

She stopped to buy a Bath bun. It was a sweet roll, far richer than the Lunn's bun according to a group of women in front of her. This bun had a lump of sugar that was baked into the bun at the bottom and sugar sprinkled on top after baking. It was divine.

To get her sweet and savory fix, she also tried one of Oliver's biscuits. It was like a hard cracker make of butter, yeast, flour, and milk and served with cheese. Talk about delicious.

Jane was glad the beach was over twenty miles away. The sight of the beach no longer filled her with delight. Now it only brought sadness and anger. She hated it. There was the sand, it got everywhere and itched. The waves made her nervous, like at any moment they would crash ashore and flood everything. Okay, so maybe she'd watched too many movies, even so, it could happen.

There was also the heat. A former sun worshipper, now she hated hot weather. Give her sweaters, scarves, hot chocolate, and boots, but no, she had to live in sunny California, the land of sunshine and waves.

Did she surf? Everyone asked when they found out where she was from. No way. No matter how many times her parents asked, Jane rarely gave in. She was happy playing at the edge of the shore or going in the water up to her thighs. Occasionally, she'd go if her dad asked enough but she never cared for the sport. Too many bad things could happen.

Jane shuddered, remembering when she was five or six and her friends had talked her into surfing. She knew how, she just didn't like it. And that day? A shark swam alongside her, bumping her board before swimming away. After that, she refused to surf again.

No matter what her mom said, she refused to go out again, gave away the board from her dad, and spent her time swimming in their pool. In the pool, you could see your feet, all the way to the bottom and knew what was lurking about, waiting to nibble your toes or break your board, not to mention your body. It was safe in the pool.

The worst part about the beach? Her father, a surfing legend, died surfing during one of the biggest storms of the century. How could her mother keep surfing after that had happened? They held the funeral at the beach. Ever since then, Jane refused to set foot on the sand. The thought of getting in the water gave her a panic attack. She'd tried several times and couldn't do it.

She made her way to the baths, joining a tour that was just leaving. Two women in front of her were talking about the tour, apparently there'd been some scandal and their friend had gotten off the tour the day before with some older man she'd met.

There was so much history Jane swore she could feel it in the very air around them. It was easy to imagine the Romans enjoying the water. And of course, Jane Austen.

As she trailed the group down the steps to the baths, she ran her fingers along the stone. Even with all the tourists taking selfies to post to social media, so consumed with getting the perfect shot, they missed enjoying the baths. It was peaceful here, as if time had stopped. The feeling grew stronger when the torches surrounding the Great Bath were lit. Her phone buzzed. 4 o'clock, time to go.

People were in a festive mood, enjoying the market and shopping. Jane loved the holidays, but she especially adored Christmas. If only she had someone to spend it with. The last few boyfriends, were, well, they lacked that swoon-worthy feeling she wanted more than anything. Her friends told her she was too picky, that not all boyfriends could be the hero in the movie, but Jane disagreed. What was love if not swoon-worthy?

The last one had been more interested in hanging out with his friends than spending time with her. The one before that hit on her mom, and the one before him was perfectly content to let her pay for everything while he tried to be a surfing pro, and thought that because she was the daughter of a famous surfer could help him with connections, no matter her dad had died last year in a surfing accident during a storm.

Her phone dinged again. The message told her to meet in an alcove. Before she could ask which alcove, she spied a shifty-looking guy in the alcove to her right, a tattered rolling suitcase next to his feet.

"I'm Jane. Here to pick up the water."

"Shh."

He put a finger to his lips, glaring at her, though no one was paying attention to them. The man unzipped the suitcase to show her the three jugs of water, then held out his hand.

"How do I know these aren't from the tap?"

With a huff, the man opened one jug, holding it up to her nose. The water was fizzing and smelled like eggs. Yuck.

"Forget I asked."

She handed over the cash. He zipped up the suitcase and showed her to a lift so she didn't have to carry the suitcase up all those steps.

By the time she dragged the suitcase, the wheels bumping

over the stones to meet the car, her phone chimed again. Thankfully, it wasn't Josie, who must still be under the influence of cold medicine.

It was the car service. The car had broken down outside of London and with a big event taking place; they didn't have another car. Jane texted back and told them not to worry, she'd take the bus back to London.

Luckily, the two women from the tour overheard her and offered her the empty seat their friend had left on the charter bus. Delighted, she accepted, buying them all a bun before they boarded. This time Jane purchased Sally Lunn buns. They were plain in appearance but big, almost six inches across with a squishy rounded top and light like brioche.

Instead of letting the driver stow the precious suitcase, she brought it onboard, refusing to let it out of her sight. If she lost the supposedly magical water, Josie would make it her mission to see that Jane never worked in Hollywood again.

As annoying as her boss could be, Jane hoped there weren't any brain-eating amoebas in the water like that poor girl back in the seventies. As awful as Josie was, she didn't wish her to die in pursuit of a magical cure.

The bus had extra empty seats, so she had two seats to herself, one for her and one for the suitcase.

A guy in the next row, leaned over and sniffed his girlfriend's hair, reminding Jane of the most disgusting task she'd performed thus far during her tenure with Josie.

Revolted by the sight, she reached for the seatbelt.
"Ouch."

A spot of blood welled up on her pinky finger from the

sharp edge on the broken seatbelt clasp. As she searched for a tissue in her backpack, Jane thought about what had to be hands down the worst day of all the awful days she'd experienced working for Josie. But no matter how awful, she'd promised her mom she wouldn't quit, that she would see the job through. So she would.

Her boss demanded Jane sniff her armpits to see if she smelled like body odor before she met her latest boyfriend, the lead singer of a rock band. Who in Jane's opinion wouldn't notice what Josie smelled like since most of the time he was drunk, high, or hadn't showered in a week, saying that too much showering washed all the natural oils off his skin.

She shuddered. The guy was attractive in that rock star, fully tattooed, bad boy way. Totally not her type. Give her a quiet, bookish guy any day.

"Sorry, everyone, there's a detour ahead so we'll be getting back a bit later than scheduled."

The gentle rain had turned into a full-blown thunderstorm, thunder booming and lightning crackling, making Jane's hair twitch.

Sighs and grumbling filled the air as the bus turned off the main road, onto what looked suspiciously like a cow path rather than a road. Worried about the water leaking, Jane leaned over to unzip the suitcase and check the jugs, when everything went haywire.

There was a crack of thunder, then a loud bang. The bus tilted to one side as glass rained down in slow motion. Screams filled the surrounding air, the smell of copper made her swallow convulsively until she was sure she wouldn't lose it.

The storm came out of nowhere, lightning, booming thunder, rain sheeting down so hard she couldn't see out the window. No matter where she looked, all Jane saw was the ocean and a tiny figure surfing on top of the biggest wave she'd ever seen.

Over and over she screamed, "Dad. Dad, please come back."

But it was too late, her dad was never coming back. The bus groaned, the muddy road giving way as the bus slid on its side straight into the water as metal screamed, people shrieked and cried out, the scent of something burning filled the air, covering up the clean smell of the countryside. Then everything went cold and dark.

4

It was so cold. Jane came to, choking on icy water as she flailed in the lake. With every stroke, the worst day of her life replayed over and over, in front of her eyes. The enormous wave, her father surfing on top, umbrellas torn away from spectators, tumbling end over end across the sands, the crowds going wild braving the storm to see her famous father surf the biggest wave in a hundred years.

Shocked cries when he wiped out. Then stunned silence when the board popped up, broken in two. The howling of the wind drowned out her own anguished screams.

Her dad didn't surface.

Hours later they recovered his body. Her mother found comfort knowing he'd died doing what he loved. As he'd wished, she cremated him and scattered his ashes in the ocean they'd loved all their lives. Her mom told Jane when her time came, she wanted the same farewell.

The relentless ocean. The place Jane couldn't get enough of until that day. Ever since then, she'd shake and everything would spin when she tried to go in the water. It had gotten so bad that thinking of that day could bring on a panic attack.

Swallowing back the fear, willing herself to think, Jane dug her nails into her palms, letting the frigid water cool the tempest within.

For a moment she wanted to float, forget everything and just watch the rain falling on the water, to remember how much she loved the feeling of being held in the water as she floated on the surface.

"Get a hold of yourself. Move or you'll freeze."

Teeth chattering, Jane struggled to make it to safety, her limbs heavy and growing heavier with every stroke, the last bit of adrenaline propelling her to land.

It wasn't until she dragged herself, soaked and shivering, onto the shore, half in and half out of the water that she realized what was missing.

There weren't any screams, not a single person in the water, and no bus. Unless the lake was deep enough that she couldn't see the bus? But the driver said the lake was shallow, only a few feet here. Something dragged her into the water. She tried to stand, went under, came up sputtering, and closed her eyes.

"Please. Make it go away."

But when she opened her eyes, she was alone. There wasn't a single sign of the crash. She looked up as an involuntary sound escaped.

Where was the road?

Why weren't there any cars or emergency vehicles?

Where was everyone?

Her backpack was somewhere at the bottom of the lake, as was the magical water Josie sent her to fetch. A half laugh half hiccup escaped as Jane knew she was now free. After this disaster, Josie would fire her for sure. It was too bad about the backpack, she could have used a snack and the wonderful hand warmers.

Would the authorities even let her leave the country since her passport and other identification, not to mention her wallet and money were now at the bottom of the lake?

Surely a diver could find her belongings? She swallowed again, thinking of the people floating, suspended in the depths of the icy waters. Shaking her head to dispel the images, Jane berated herself for not wearing the red sweater instead of the ivory. Rescuers would see red easier.

Thoughts floated in and out of her mind as she pulled herself the rest of the way out of the water, inch by agonizing inch, the scent of seawater strong in her nose and hair.

That was odd. No matter how she tried, she couldn't figure out why the lake smelled like the ocean or her mom's hair. Her mom always smelled like the beach, making it hard sometimes for Jane to hug her. The scent permeated the house until she could no longer stand it, had to get away from California and the lingering memories.

Exhausted, she decided to rest for a moment before going for help.

Unsure of how much time had passed, Jane smiled up at the silver sky. At least the storm was over.

No longer cold, a small smile crept across her face as the first snowflake hit her nose.

"It's snowing."

The flakes were delicate and cold, like something out of a dream. It was so quiet. The snow muffled everything around her. She tried to reach up and touch a snowflake but couldn't seem to lift her arms, so she stayed where she was, content to watch the snow fall, covering up the shore. It was even more beautiful than in the movies.

"They're all perfect."

Perhaps if she went back in the water she could find a passageway and swim back to California? Though why did the lake smell like the ocean?

A tiny part of her brain was screaming at her that she was freezing to death and delirious, while the fanciful part of her brain decided she was a fish and could easily swim all the way back home. There was no need to be afraid of the ocean any longer, not when she was a fish.

⚜

NICHOLAS RODE WITH A SMALL CONTINGENT OF MEN TO Winterborne. He spent a se'nnight at his eldest brother's keep, availing himself of the fine furnishings and fully stocked larder whilst repairs were made to his own home after the fire. The stables along with a few other outbuildings had burned to the ground. That was why he preferred stone instead of wood for building.

If 'twas the only coincidence since he had arrived at his

home, Nicholas would have dismissed the fire, certain some careless servant started the blaze.

However, he had narrowly avoided being crushed when several stones fell from the battlements, barely missing his head. Someone had chiseled away the mortar, meaning an enemy wished him ill. But why?

Another day, he had been hunting in the woods when an arrow embedded itself in the tree where he had only moments before been leaning. If he had not bent over to pick up something shiny embedded in the leaves, Nicholas would have taken an arrow to the face. Without thinking about it, he rubbed the ancient gold and emerald ring he'd found in the forest that day. Mayhap it had belonged to a long ago king or warrior?

In his score and five years, Nicholas had made enemies, but then again, who had not? But someone who wished him dead? He did not know who, but he would find out. Until he knew who and why, no one rode alone. His brother, Alfred, wondered if it could be their cousin who Nicholas had dismissed as steward of Winterborne, but the man was a coward, more likely to use poison like a woman.

He was halfway home when a messenger met them on the path. The man stopped, opened his cloak and lifted his worn tunic to show he did not have the pestilence. The colder it turned, the fewer people died.

"My lord." The man dug through his bag and came up with a tattered missive.

Nicholas gave the messenger a few coins for his trouble before the man rode away.

"Rest the horses."

He looked up at the silver sky.

"Then we needs go for 'twill soon snow and I wish to be seated in front of the fire, a cup of spiced wine in my hand before nightfall."

He dismounted and sat on the ground, his cloak under him as he frowned, seeing the seal. 'Twas from Portugal, from Monsieur Silva. He was a wealthy merchant with five ships to his name. Nicholas would soon be a very wealthy man, thanks to the enormous dowry that accompanied his daughter on her voyage.

The letter was brief. There was illness spreading across the lands, stormy seas, and several ports were closed, so the ship would anchor off the coast near Winterborne. A small skiff would bring Jane to him, along with several servants, her dowry, and three horses.

The letter was dated a month ago. There had been a powerful storm not long after the letter was written and again last night. A group of traveling minstrels they encountered told of terrible shipwrecks, loss of lives and goods, and how so many died they were now being buried in pits.

"Make haste." He called to the men, telling Sir Cedric of the letter as they galloped towards home. Perchance his intended was already there waiting for him?

Winterborne was on the west coast of England, twenty-five miles from Bath and across the Bristol Channel from Wales.

They rode hard until late in the day when the snow fell. Not long after, one of the men called out.

Nicholas reined in his horse as he looked to the cove.

"Merde."

Wreckage from a large ship lay scattered across the sands, but 'twas the tattered scrap of color that caught his eye. The flag of Portugal.

"Saints be." He dismounted and made his way down the path to the shore.

Two of his men met him on the sand.

"Is she here? Where is Jane?"

"Nay. We have found none alive."

The man swallowed.

"We searched each body. They did not have the sickness." The man crossed himself.

The sea and the wind could be fearsome, especially in winter. He nodded, lips pressed tight as he scanned the churning waters.

"We will see them buried at Winterborne."

No longer in a hurry, he strode over to a lad from the stables.

"They are calm now, my lord."

The lad patted the horse then nodded to two other boys who were shivering in the early snow.

"We found the three of them wandering about. Shall we take them home?"

The sight of the tattered flag and the three horses promised in Jane's dowry, told the truth of what had happened.

"Aye, see them to the stables, feed and water them."

Once home, he would send a letter to her sire, telling him of the storm and the loss of his only daughter.

William, his captain, and the most fierce warrior Nicholas had ever fought alongside, approached.

"There are no survivors. 'Twas a ferocious storm last night, Godric said part of the chapel roof collapsed. They did not know your intended was arriving or would have met the ship."

Nicholas let out a breath.

"Salvage what you can and take the lads home. I do not think we will see much snow but we do not want any taking ill."

He strode along, speaking to the men and servants as they cleaned up the wreckage. They could use most of what they found for other purposes, the sea would take the rest.

As he reached the far side of the cove, a bit of cloth fluttered in the wind. A tattered scrap of blue silk. When he was almost to the rocks, he caught sight of a battered wooden chest and was that... yes, 'twas a foot, and boots unlike any he had ever seen.

'Twas a lad, dressed in hose and an ivory tunic of fine wool, unlike any he had ever seen. Portugal had fine wares indeed.

Nicholas tossed the broken boards off the lad, blinking. 'Twas not a lad at all, but a gel. He sat back on his heels. The pale face, unblemished skin, and slender form.

'Twas his Jane.

Why had his intended dressed as a lad? Mayhap 'twas how they traveled? Odd customs to be sure.

"Demoiselle?"

She did not stir.

"Jane?"

Her skin was so cold to his touch. Snow fell on her face. Her skin was soft, the palest marble, lips a faint blue, and lashes dark. He wanted her to open her eyes, for he wished to know what color they were. In the miniature they were light but he had an urgent need to know.

Nicholas scooped her up in his arms, careful not to jostle her as water ran down his tunic and hose. She was so cold, like holding a woman made of snow and ice. He had to warm her.

She stirred, a small cry escaped as she blinked slowly up at him.

"It's so cold."

She let out a soft sigh, her breath cold against his face.

"You're pretty. You must be the hero in the book I've been reading."

His intended patted his arm and closed her eyes again, turning her face to his tunic, seeking the warmth he offered.

It took Nicholas several moments to decipher the words. She was not speaking Portuguese but some low-born form of English. Was this what she had been taught?

Merde.

He tried again.

"Jane. Jane, you must wake."

His betrothed did not answer as he bellowed for his horse.

5

The accident and aftermath came in flashes.

Jane wasn't sure what was real and what was fantasy. The accident seemed real but then again, so did a guy who was as comfortable with a sword as a businessman was with a phone.

Warmth curled around her as she floated.

A deep, warm, velvety voice called her name as if she were the most precious thing in the world to him.

Strong arms held her tight.

The smell of horses and leather, the forest in winter, and a hint of freshly cut grass filled the air.

The lulling motion of riding, a memory from childhood overlaid with her as an adult, wet and scared.

When she finally woke, thoughts muddled, she found herself in a bed, burrowed into the warmth, the bed swaying slightly as she moved.

Ever so slowly, she blinked again. Wait, a minute. This wasn't her hotel. Was she in the hospital?

She shook her head and winced, holding still until the dizziness subsided.

No, this was no hospital. It was some kind of medieval-looking bedroom.

Oh. Right.

The accident.

Had they found her fellow passengers? Had Josie found out what had happened? Jane reached for her ever-present phone, then stopped. She was no longer wearing her wet clothes, but some kind of long linen shirt.

She looked around the room, slowly, until she was sure she would not faint.

Maybe someone had taken her to a nearby historic house? For a moment she thought she was on the set, back in London, at the castle. Though if she was, why wasn't Josie standing here screeching at her? At least she didn't have to listen to her now ex-boss.

The room was rustic in its simplicity, yet beautiful with its whitewashed walls, stunning tapestries, and sturdy wooden bed. Jane relaxed in the bed that almost needed a step to reach the floor. The stone floors looked new instead of worn down by centuries of feet traipsing across them. There was a sturdy-looking chair in front of the fire though no sofas or other upholstered furniture.

Someone obviously liked the idea of living in the past. These must be reproductions of antiques because they looked new instead of old and battered. It took her a moment to wriggle out of the covers and work herself up to a sitting position using the pillows to prop her up in the masculine bed.

Memories floated through her mind then vanished. Why had the lake smelled like the ocean? Even now she could smell the faint tang of salty air, swore she could hear the faint sound of the treacherous waves.

It hurt to think. Warmth filled the room making her sleepy. A fire with actual genuine wood, not electric or gas, blazed in an enormous working hearth carved with stags, fruit, and some kind of crest.

Jane closed her eyes, slowly turned her head to look at the other side of the room, opened them, and froze.

There in a chair across from the bed was a man. How had she missed him? Even in sleep he filled the space with his presence. The guy had broad shoulders. He stretched his long legs out in front of him, arms crossed over his chest. Dark hair hung down to his shoulders, his chin rested on his chest as he slept. He dressed in costume in a black tunic and hose and wore a sword and several daggers on his person, along with a small battered pouch that hung from his waist. His boots looked like they'd seen better days though they were very authentic looking.

When she opened her mouth to ask what he was doing here, not a single sound emerged. Jane tried again, but the words wouldn't come. He stirred, mumbled something and was quiet again.

Talk about a dream.

Seeing him, made things clear. He had to be the new leading actor starring in the movie with Josie. The guy looked like someone had carved him from a block of marble. There were laugh lines at the corners of his eyes. It looked like he hadn't shaved in a few days, and she wondered if his eyes might be green or maybe hazel?

Guys like him never looked twice at average girls like her. So why was he here? Maybe she hadn't been fired, and Josie sent him to keep an eye on her until she could fire Jane in person, as one bright red nail tapped against the crystal encrusted cup she carried everywhere, just like the famous singer she admired.

Whoever called this guy their boyfriend, sure was lucky to have him. Then again, being with a guy that good-looking had to be nerve-wracking. Who wanted a boyfriend that was prettier than you?

What was she forgetting? Jane frowned, thinking. A log popped in the hearth and she jumped.

That was it. The absence of noise. It was quiet. Too quiet. The bubbled glass in the window obscured the view as she strained to see from the bed, listening for the ring of a cellphone, the rev of an engine, the director yelling cut. But there was nothing other than the storm.

Wind rattled the glass, and she relaxed. They'd probably stopped filming outside for the day because of the weather. The walls were stone, they likely muffled most sound that was why she couldn't hear the crew moving about.

The scuff of a boot on stone made her jerk her gaze back to her babysitter, even as he and the room spun in slow lazy circles.

"Demoiselle? My lady Jane, are you unwell?"

His lady? How did he know her name? Despair flowed through her. Josie must have told him to watch her until she could tear into Jane.

While she was pondering the thought, he went to the hearth, came back and handed her a cup. It was warm in her hands, the scent of spiced wine filled her nose as she sipped. She took another sip. When she looked up at him, the room had stopped spinning.

"It's you."

He had green eyes, the color of moss. When he smiled, it was like the sun streamed through the windows banishing the storm.

The guy paused a moment as if translating her words.

"Aye. Do you remember what happened?"

Jane sipped the warm wine as she thought about everything that had happened. When she looked into his eyes, she saw such kindness it was almost her undoing.

"I was in an accident. We went into the water. Where are the others?"

She clenched the blanket in one fist as she stared into space; the horror returning.

"I didn't see anyone else or the bus. It must be at the bottom of the lake."

He frowned.

"Bus? I know not this word."

Then he leaned over, the scent of the forest enveloping her as he touched the back of his hand to her forehead.

"No fever. 'Tis well."

He took the cup and went to a small stool by the hearth, where he refilled their wine.

"Drink. You were cold as the snow when I found you. Saints be, you are most fortunate to be alive."

Why me? She wanted to ask but didn't voice the words for fear of hearing the answer. To give herself time to think, she took the cup from him and sipped, letting the warmth work its way through her veins.

"Did Josie send you to watch me? I'm fine. Really, I'll deal with it, but no therapists, no matter what she says. I should get back to work."

She tried to get out of bed as the room spun, and before she knew it, he'd taken the cup, set it down then tucked the covers around her so tightly she couldn't move.

"Nay. You must rest."

He watched her as she looked around the room.

"Do not worry, we are betrothed so 'tis proper for me to see to your well-being."

He paused a moment. "Your lady's maid and the other servants perished in the storm. I will have someone from Winterborne serve you if it pleases you."

Knowing better than to shake her head, Jane replayed his words.

It was odd, he'd somehow known her name but called her his fiancee. No, that wasn't the word.

His *betrothed*.

"The other passengers... are you sure they didn't make it?" Her hand trembled. "I'm the only survivor?"

"Aye. You and the horses. And your dowry."

He took her hand in his.

"You are more beautiful than your portrait."

At her blank look, he crossed the room and came back with a small fabric wrapped parcel. It was a miniature painting of a woman. She peered at it. The woman's hair was covered, her face generic enough that Jane along with lots of other women, could have easily passed for her. But how did he know her name?

She handed him back the tiny portrait.

"You called me Jane. How do you know my name?"

He frowned. "We are betrothed. Why would I not know your name? You are Jane Silva from Portugal."

He tapped one booted foot against the stone.

"I will send a letter to your sire, he needs know what has transpired."

"My father is dead."

Jane blinked, trying to stay awake. It was cozy in the room; he smelled amazing, and the wine had worked its way through her system.

"My name is Jane Randall and I'm from California not Portugal. I think Josie must be playing a joke on you."

She yawned.

"But great job staying in character. I wish I was in the movie. I'd drag you to the altar so fast your head would spin."

And with that she passed out, the sound of masculine laughter filling the air.

WHEN JANE WOKE AGAIN, SHE WAS STILL IN THE SUMPTUOUS room. From the light coming through the window, she wondered if she'd slept through the night.

"So it wasn't a dream."

She sat up and looked around. The drop-dead gorgeous actor was gone. Likely off to inform Josie that she was awake so her boss could berate her before firing her in person.

There was a bit of bread and cheese, along with a cup of water on a stool next to the bed. Suddenly ravenous, she ate, drank the icy cold water, and took stock of herself.

Every part of her body ached. Her hair was crunchy, her skin tight, and her clothes nowhere to be found. She was wearing what might have been one of the actor's costume shirts. Her face burned as she wondered if he'd been the one to remove her wet clothes?

No, probably the women from the costume department or a doctor had done it. Jane took her time getting out of bed, waited a minute and when the room didn't spin, walked over to the window seat, looked out and nodded. Maybe lunch time? Or early afternoon? So she had slept through the rest of the day and the night. No wonder she felt better. The accident was quiet for a change, not playing over and over in her head.

There were actors out in the courtyard, though things looked nothing like they had before. Maybe they'd changed the set?

Unwilling to wait for Josie, Jane looked down. The shirt went to mid-thigh, kind of like a mini dress which normally would have been fine. But it would be cold and damp in the corridors, so she grabbed a blanket from the bed, wrapped it around herself like a toga and pulled the heavy door open, resolved to quit before Josie could fire her. Once it was done, she'd go back to the hotel, pack her things, checkout, and go look at the cottage she'd found online. Then she'd... turn off her cellphone for the first time in ages.

Everything would work out fine.

❧ 6 ❧

Nicholas bent over, hands on his knees, panting, in the brisk air. Another year almost gone and still he was not wed.

Alfred and his wife were expecting another child, given how little time they spent together, Nicholas wanted to commend his brother. Nay, he did not wish to wait another year to wed, two long years was enough, 'twas long past time to see the deed done.

Saints be praised Jane did not have the illness that was sweeping across the lands.

He stalked over to the well in the courtyard, pulled up a bucket, drank deeply, then dumped the rest over his head, shaking like his favorite dogs after they jumped in the water.

"Nick, you needs make haste. Your betrothed is, er... she is dressed..." His captain's face turned bright red as he pointed.

"What the bloody hell?"

Nicholas narrowed his eyes as his betrothed glided across the courtyard, barefoot and wrapped in his favorite blanket.

Servants crossed themselves, several men whistled and made lewd comments that had Nicholas scowling as he marked each man. When one of the garrison knights caught sight of him, he elbowed the two men with him, turning pale, they scurried off to the battlements. It made no difference. He turned back to William.

"Egbert, Jacob, and Paul. They will meet me in the lists after dinner."

His captain grinned.

"Aye, them and any others who dare to gaze upon the lady." The man who had been at his side for a year said under his breath, "though 'tis quite a sight to see."

Nicholas smiled on the inside.

His Jane only came up to his shoulders. She was beautiful with long wavy hair, hazel eyes, and a smooth, unmarked face. Nicholas winced as she spoke, the language difficult to understand. It sounded as if she were searching for someone named Josie. Was this Josie her lady's maid, or mayhap another servant who perished in the storm?

The servant shook his head, backing away, as his betrothed shivered, looking lost.

Halfway to her, he stopped. Why was she not speaking her own tongue? Come to think on it, she had not uttered one word of Portuguese since he had found her. 'Twas most vexing.

"Oh, it's you."

She smiled up at him, making Nicholas catch his breath.

He gestured at her.

"Might we find you more suitable... er... clothing?"

His betrothed looked down, then shrugged as if 'twas normal to wear a blanket from the bed as clothing.

"I couldn't find my clothes."

She waved a hand in the air as the blanket shifted, baring her legs to the knees. Saints she had fetching ankles and shapely legs.

Nicholas scowled at the men who quickly went about their business. He would run through any who did not show the proper respect no matter how odd his soon-to-be bride.

"Anyway, where I come from this is totally covered up. You should see some of the bikinis at the beach near my house, they're really more like string, holding tiny bits of fabric over the—"

She turned a fetching shade of pink. "Over, well, you know."

He grinned, arching a brow.

"Nay. Pray tell, as I am unfamiliar with your customs. I find I should like to hear more of this bi-kin-i."

He offered his arm, deliriously happy when her skin deepened from pink to red.

She took his arm, then stopped, looking at him.

"I still don't know your name."

He frowned, wondering if she had hit her head when she went overboard, as he made her a small bow.

"Nicholas Montgomery, Lord Winterborne, *a seu serviço*."

"Nice to meet you. Thank you so much for rescuing me."

She wrinkled her nose, looking like a rabbit scenting the air.

"What was that you were saying? Something about service? Why are you speaking a different language?" Then she muttered under her breath, "as if this isn't strange enough as it is."

He wholeheartedly agreed with her.

She made a face as if tasting or smelling something foul.

"I thought this movie was supposed to be set around the time of King Henry. Off with their heads and all that?"

When he only blinked at her, she huffed out a breath and stomped off towards his hall, leaving him gaping after her.

Movies? King Henry?

Nicholas caught up to her and offered his arm again.

"Edward the third is King of England."

Before she could stop again and trip him, she stumbled and cried out.

"Ouch, that hurt."

He was an unchivalrous dolt.

"Your feet must be freezing." He swept her up in his arms as she let out a squeak.

"What are you doing? I can walk."

"Nay. You are barefoot and there are sharp stones which could cut your tender feet."

"Well, then."

She turned pink again.

"That's so nice of you. No one's ever carried me before."

His intended patted his arm.

"Am I terribly heavy? Working in Hollywood really messes with your sense of reality when it comes to the female form."

Nicholas remembered when Alfred's wife was heavy with child and Alfred told her she was bigger than the pig the cook had slaughtered that morn. He would not fall into the same trap.

"Nay. You are light as a bird. I admire your form, 'Tis most pleasing."

She turned the color of the sunset.

He carried her up the steps, kicking the doors to the hall open as it started to rain again.

"Bring clothes, food, and drink for my lady," he bellowed as he took the steps two at a time up to his solar.

One man scurried to open the door, then quickly shut it behind Nicholas when he saw the look on his face.

"You will warm yourself, then we shall eat."

He settled her in the chair by the fire, pulled a stool over and sat in front of her.

"I have questions."

She snorted. "No kidding, so do I."

He inclined his head.

"The lady shall go first."

Before she could ask him anything, servants entered bearing heavily laden trays.

"Food and wine for you, my lord. And clothes for your lady. We laundered what washed up on the beach."

The older serving woman crossed herself.

"And the odd garments she was wearing when you found her."

Servants were a superstitious lot.

"See to a bath for Jane. She is chilled."

He shut his mouth before he said her feet were as filthy as a peasant.

The servants left them to the food, shutting the door behind them so they would not be disturbed. She was looking around his solar as if she had never seen a place such as Winterborne. Was her home so different? Might she not care for his home?

Nicholas prepared her a plate, choosing the best morsels, brought her wine, then did the same for himself.

"We will sup. Then we will have speech."

"It looks very good."

There was bread, wine, a hearty beef stew, chicken, and pie.

There were dark circles under her eyes, her skin pale as the moon. She was quiet as she ate, lost in her own thoughts. He finished, set the plate on the floor and waited as he watched her.

Once she finished eating, she took a deep breath almost as if she did not wish to hear answers to her questions.

"Did the script change to medieval England?"

She held up two fingers.

"Are you the lead? Where are my clothes? Where is my phone? Where is Josie?"

She swallowed. "She's going to have my head," she muttered.

Then she straightened in the chair.

"The castle looks different. Where are we? Why did you

speak another language to me? Why are people speaking some kind of weird French? And why on earth do you keep calling me your betrothed?"

A harsh breath escaped as she slumped in the chair, her toes dangerously close to the fire.

He jumped up, moved her chair back far enough so she would not burn her feet, then he sat, and deciding he needed it, drained the wine. When she looked at him, he nodded at the cups.

"Please."

Grateful to have something to do, he refilled their cups, bringing another blanket to cover her.

Nicholas let out a breath.

"I will answer your questions and then you will answer mine. Agreed?"

She nodded.

"I do not know what is a *script*. We are in England at my home. Winterborne Castle."

He watched her to see if she would faint. When she did not, he continued.

"Aye, I am the leader. Lord Winterborne. The castle is mine to command. As we are betrothed, you may call me Nicholas. Your traveling clothes were most odd. Why were you dressed as a lad?"

He held up a hand.

"Do not answer. I will wait until 'tis my turn."

He ran a hand through his hair.

"I do not know what is a *phone*. If this Josie was your maid or servant..."

He hesitated a moment.

"None survived the shipwreck. She is dead."

His Jane opened, then shut her mouth. She wrapped her arms around her middle.

Nicholas continued.

"Portuguese is the language of your country, is it not?"

He held up a hand.

"You arrived by ship with your servants, three horses, and a rather large dowry as we are to be wed and have been promised to each other for two long years."

Satisfied he had answered her questions, Nicholas relaxed. He knew from Alfred's wife 'twas important to listen to his woman, to let her say what she wished when they were alone. The candles burned low as they talked and ate.

She had been twisting a lock of her hair round and round her fingers while staring into the fire.

"Josie was my boss. She's one of the most famous actors in the world. I dressed in what I always wear when it's cold outside. I wasn't on a boat, I was on a bus and we crashed and ended up in a lake. Yes, my name is Jane, but it's Jane Randall from California. Half a dozen women look like that portrait you showed me. I do not know who you are, I have never met you, and think I would know if I were engaged."

She sniffed.

"Even way out here in the country you should know about movies. And Edward whoever isn't king. England had a queen, Elizabeth, who reigned a very long time. She recently passed away. Now her son, Charles, is King of England."

Mayhap her father thought to send a witless gel to him, no

wonder her dowry was so large. To believe a woman ruled England. Nicholas snorted. His mother would have made a good queen, but he did not know this Elizabeth or Charles.

"Jane?"

"Yes?" She blinked at him.

"When you left your home had many perished from the Great Pestilence?"

At the look upon her face, he held out his hands.

"None of the sailors nor servants on the ship were ill, none had the black marks on their skin. My men looked at the bodies before we buried them at Winterborne. I will show you where when you are feeling better so you may pray over them."

Her eyes widened, and if 'twas possible she turned even paler than before.

"Do you mean the *Black Plague?*"

He pursed his lips, thinking.

"Nay, I have not heard it called thus, but mayhap in your land 'tis how it is known. The king's own daughter was struck down."

His intended was muttering to herself.

"How can it be? I don't believe in magic. It isn't possible. The plague. Just great."

Nicholas frowned. She was turning green. Before she toppled over, he swept her up in his arms.

"What are you doing?" Her eyes were huge, sweat beaded on her brow.

"Breathe. In and out. You have had a fright."

He sat in the chair, settling her on his lap, making sure he wrapped the blanket around her so she would not catch a chill.

"Do you need the chamber pot? If you are going to be ill, I will hold your hair until the servant returns."

"How very gallant of you. No, I think I'm okay."

She shrugged.

"You keep saying we're to be married, but this is the first time I've ever laid eyes on you. Shouldn't you know what the woman you're going to marry looks like?"

"Nay, our sire's arranged the match. We did not meet until you arrived here at Winterborne."

He frowned.

"Where is California? Is it in Portugal?"

She blinked at him as if he were a rather dim child.

"California is in America. I'm not from Portugal."

Nicholas patted her shoulder.

"Your belly is full. You will have a bath, dress in warm clothes, take a turn about the grounds, and then you will sleep well tonight. My mother believes sleep to be healing. The shipwreck must have addled your wits and you do not remember whence you came or that we are to wed. I will write to your father and you will read the letter. Do not fret. All will be well."

She let out a soft cry.

"Is aught amiss?" Nicholas wiped the wetness from her cheeks. Forlorn eyes met his, the anguish in them piercing his heart.

"You don't understand. My father died last year."

7

What on earth was going on? The actual *Black Plague*?

Jane didn't know whether to laugh hysterically or scream at the top of her lungs to wake up. The only explanation was that she was in the hospital in a coma, and because she was sleep deprived from working for Josie on a movie that was set in the past, that somehow her brain had conjured up this reality while her body healed.

Nicholas patted her shoulder, bringing her back to the present. He told her not to worry, the horrors of what she had witnessed, losing her servants in the storm, battling the ferocious waves, had addled her wits.

Servants?

He'd settled her in the chair, tucked a blanket around her, then went to the door and bellowed.

Servants scurried to do his bidding.

Jane would have to remember that trick. It seemed bellowing worked wonders for getting what you wanted.

Before she knew it, servants heated water over the fire. From behind a screen in the room's corner, they brought out a deep, padded, wooden tub. An older woman produced a small clump of honey scented soap along with a rag for washing, and a comb to work the tangles out of her hair. She set them on a low wooden stool beside the tub.

While Nicholas talked, the women filled the tub with hot water, until steam filled the air, making her sleepy.

He nodded to the women.

"I shall take my leave of you."

At the door to the chamber, he paused, turned to her. "After your bath would you care to walk with me? I could show you the grounds of Winterborne."

"I'd like that."

Might as well get a good look at the place. Who knew she had such a vivid imagination?

Good job conjuring up the actual perfect book boyfriend.

With a nod he left, the room emptier without him.

The women offered to help her wash, but that was too much for Jane. Instead, she smiled and said she would do it herself in honor of losing her trusted servants. Seemed she'd learned a thing or two about acting from Josie after all.

They gave her a cloth to dry off, laid her clothes by the fire and left her to soak. A bath by the fire was nice. The cottage she'd looked at online had a fireplace in the bathroom. Not to mention running water, flushing toilets, refrigerators and stores nearby full of lovely groceries, anything she could possibly want.

What if she was wrong, and she wasn't in the hospital? But was *elsewhere?*

Would her mother hold a service on the water for her as well? Fall apart like she had? Jane splashed a bit of the water against the side of the tub. No, her mom was one of the strongest people Jane knew. She'd survive the loss.

It was Jane who was weak. Who couldn't get past what had happened to her as a child and losing her dad. No matter how hard she tried, the ocean held sway over her.

With a shake of her head, she pushed the thoughts down deep, until it didn't hurt so much, instead focusing on her current state of affairs. Last night and today had been surreal.

Before Nicholas left, he said that after they returned from their walk, they would have supper in the great hall so the people could meet their new lady. Everyone thought she was Jane from Portugal. It had to be more than a coincidence that she and the other woman shared the same name.

With a roll of her eyes, she went under the water. She did not believe in fate or magic. There was a logical explanation, she just didn't know what it was. At least not yet.

Was the other Jane at the bottom of the ocean along with everyone else from the shipwreck and the bus passengers?

When she could no longer hold her breath, Jane surfaced, water running down her face, the heat from the fire turning her skin pink. The steam rose around her as she leaned against the padded edge of the tub thinking about what she knew.

She had left Bath, the water for Josie in her possession on the charter bus, when they were caught in a terrible thunderstorm. The bus lost control or something broke and they wrecked, landing in the lake. But somehow she'd wound up on a beach amidst a shipwreck with no survivors and everyone dressed like they were on a movie set.

The people were hard to understand. There wasn't a single car or other modern convenience in sight. During her time here, she'd heard of castles where the owners left parts of the place untouched so tourists could see what it had been like to live back then. But there was rustic and then there was Winterborne.

Nicholas was part of the aristocracy but acted like he didn't know what an actor was and had never heard of Josie. Not to mention he claimed to have never heard of movies or phones.

The castle was all wrong. They weren't in London but somewhere on the coast. He thought she'd been in a shipwreck and was engaged to marry him. And he thought she was from Portugal.

Jane shifted in the water, the faint scent of honey in the air, along with the smell of warm stone, and the smoky smell from the fire. What else did she know?

He'd said Edward the third was king. When was he king? Not like she knew. Why hadn't she paid attention in history. Oh. Right. Because it was boring.

The thought slammed into her. Somehow she'd ended up in the past. But when?

It was such a ridiculous thought that she laughed out loud.

Though why didn't anyone have cell phones? The castle was beyond rustic. It was the definition of medieval, with torches in the corridors, no electricity, and no hot running water.

Wait. He'd said there was a plague, the Great Pestilence. That meant she was in medieval England. Jane wracked her brain, searching for the answer.

The water cooled, making her shiver. She hauled herself out of the tub, dried off with the cloth, then sat in front of the fire, combing her hair, working out the tangles, and thinking until she thought her head would explode.

"The fourteenth century." That was it.

"No way." She shook her head. How had she traveled through time? Why her? She was a nobody, she didn't even like history.

Once her hair was dry, she held up her leggings.

"These won't do."

They looked like what Nicholas and the other men wore. Here women wore dresses. Maybe she should see what else they brought her to wear.

She recognized a chemise, long tunic, belt, and headdress from her time on the set. The chemise, tunic, and belt were simple enough to put on, but the headdress? No way. Instead, she tied her hair back with a piece of ribbon. Where were her boots? The conversation came back to her as she remembered a young serving girl telling her they'd been lost in the storm. With a skeptical eye, she slipped on the embroidered slippers, hoping they'd keep her feet warm. They were small, but would work for now.

There was also a beautifully embroidered maroon cloak lined with some kind of fur which she'd be grateful for if it was as cold as she remembered. Why did people like cold climates? The snow and cold weather was something she wanted to visit, not live through every year.

What to do with her sweater, shirt, and leggings? Not to mention the undergarments?

Burn them. The thought came unbidden. Jane's mom strongly believed in intuition, so before she could change her mind, Jane tossed the bundle into the fire, waiting until the clothing caught fire.

"You're going to feel really stupid when you go outside and everyone is on their phones, drinking, and wearing jeans and coats."

8

Satisfied the fire had reduced the clothing to unrecognizable ashes, Jane opened the door to see two enormous dogs, tails wagging, tongues lolling. "Hello."

They scrambled to their feet, took a few steps and looked back at her as if to say, *well, come on, what are you waiting for?*

With a shrug, she followed them through the corridors, down the steps, through the great hall, ignoring all the whispers, and followed the dogs outside.

They trotted along, both of them coming almost to her hip as she followed. Maybe some kind of wolfhound?

Winterborne wasn't at all what she expected. The castle gleamed in the muted afternoon light. It was a creamy white, whitewashed and plastered over the stonework. She was staring at the side of the castle, at a protruding area with a hole when it hit her, it was a medieval bathroom. The breeze from the nearby ocean must keep the smells at bay.

You'd do your business and it would go down into the barrel. She saw a servant scrubbing the walls under a chute. Stomach turning, she walked faster. The dog nudged her, and she patted him as she stared at everything around her, looking for anything she might recognize.

These were not actors. They were going about their day-to-day lives. There were buildings that looked like they'd been damaged and rebuilt, alongside new buildings like the smithy.

Not one person had a cellphone. She looked around. There were no power lines, no planes in the sky, no cars. Not even a road that she could see. If she could get up to the battlements, then she could be sure, but worrisome thoughts of silly things like time travel kept flitting through her mind.

The sound of men laughing and shouting insults, along with the ring of steel had her craning her neck to see where it was coming from. The dogs stopped every few feet to sniff something before continuing on towards the lists.

She was almost there. The dogs had run ahead to Nicholas who'd gone down on one knee to pet them, when someone shoved her from behind.

Jane went sprawling, there was the sound of hooves and wagon wheels, and then she found herself in his arms. Again.

"Wow, how did you get to me so fast?"

He'd caught her and swung her up on a horse as if she weighed nothing.

"The horses could have crushed you beneath the wheels. Are you unharmed?" He patted her arms and legs, then realizing he was touching her legs, pulled his hands back as if she were on fire.

"I'm fine. Someone pushed me."

Nicholas narrowed his eyes. He called to one of his men, murmured to the man and sent him on his way.

"I will find out what happened. There have been odd doings of late."

She shivered.

"Stone falling from the battlements. An arrow narrowly missing my head." He shrugged.

The horse moved, and Jane flinched.

Nicholas' deep voice came next to her ear.

"You seem as if you have never seen a horse before."

When she let go of her death grip on him, she patted the horse.

"I can't ride. No one really rides horses where I come from."

"Your sire is renowned for his fine horseflesh." She heard the frown in his voice.

Jane shifted. "Perhaps, but I do not ride."

Hrumph. "Then I shall teach you."

"That would be nice."

They rode out through the gates, two men following. As they rode, Jane looked around, but no matter how far in the distance she could see there wasn't any sign of a road. No power lines. No vehicles of any kind. Nothing but countryside.

Oblivious to her rising panic, Nicholas talked about his home and the horses her father had sent, or rather the other

Jane's father.

"I have dispatched a messenger to inform your sire you survived the shipwreck and we will soon wed."

He patted her arm. "You were most vexed last night when you said your sire was dead."

She stiffened. Now was not the time, not until she knew what was going on. It was best to keep quiet.

"I guess I was hysterical from the shipwreck."

"In time, you will forget."

He was wrong. She'd never forget.

They went a bit further when he pointed to the forest. "Do not ride alone in the woods, 'tis dangerous."

She nodded as she thought about everything she'd seen thus far. The way people dressed. How comfortable he was on horseback. The castle.

There was no other explanation.

She, Jane Randall of California, a nobody, had somehow traveled through time. With no idea how she'd gotten here, and not a clue how to get back to her own time, Jane decided she'd play along until she could figure out a plan.

The Jane that Nicholas thought he was getting was dead, which gave her time to pretend to be this other woman until she could figure out how to get home.

Because as much as she wanted to believe she was in the middle of the movie being filmed on the outskirts of London, Josie was nowhere to be found and this not only looked real, but smelled real.

A small smile passed her lips at the thought of Josie.

By now, her boss must have thrown the tantrum to end all

tantrums at not getting her magic water or knowing what happened to Jane.

The water.

Jane stiffened.

Could it be?

And if so, Bath existed in this time. All she had to do was go there... and do what? It wasn't like she'd touched the waters or drank them. Her shoulders slumped.

Maybe she needed to get in the water?

Find the lake on the way from Bath and dive in?

Click her heels together three times and make a wish to go home?

She touched his hand. He stopped mid-sentence from telling her about the game in the woods.

"Nicholas?"

She heard the smile in his voice when she'd used his name.

"Aye, Jane?"

He wore a dark green tunic and hose which turned his eyes a darker green, more the color of pine trees in winter.

She shifted on the horse to watch his face when she asked.

"I was wondering... might we take a trip to Bath to take the waters before we wed?"

A smile lit up his face.

"Your wits have returned. Bath? Aye, if 'tis safe. I will find out. Why Bath, pray tell?"

What were a few white lies when she was pretending to be someone else?

"I have heard the waters are good for the skin and ensure a good marriage."

Nicholas dismounted and lifted her off the horse. The sound of the waves was louder here making her grind her teeth as she followed him.

"Aye. If the sickness has passed, we will go to Bath. There is a market there you may enjoy."

He smiled, looking younger and more carefree than he had earlier. Something was weighing on him, but she didn't know him well enough to ask.

"I shall begin wooing you."

Startled by the declaration, she coughed, and coughed some more, until Nicholas helpfully pounded her on the back, almost sending her to her knees.

"Would you rather I did not woo you?"

He peered at her as if she were the most interesting person in the world. It was a look she'd seen many men give... to Josie. But never to her. It felt... good.

"Wooing would be nice. We could get to know each other. You might want to back out of this engagement."

It was her turn to grin and show her teeth.

"Who knows, I might be a shrew or burp whenever I eat, or stay in bed drunk all day."

At the alarm on his face, she laughed out loud, startling a bird from a nearby tree,

"Don't worry... I'm not a drunk."

Nicholas blinked, unsure if she was kidding or not. Finally, he nodded.

"The men would find it most entertaining to hear you belch."

He looked at his hands as if such awful behavior didn't

bother him in the least.

"Mayhap a shrewish wife would be good. I could send you to the stables and the larder to unleash your shrewish tongue on the vermin. I wager in a fortnight they would all be gone from Winterborne."

He pulled the cloak tighter around her so she wouldn't be cold. She barely knew him, yet he was more considerate than any guy she'd ever met.

"Once I hear from your sire, we will wed."

Jane knew mail was notoriously slow, so she wasn't too worried. By then she'd be happily back in her own time, scarfing down pizza and binge watching her favorite shows.

She tasted salt on her lips as she looked over the cliffs. Without thinking, she took his hand, holding tight as she looked at the treacherous waves.

"You are trembling." He turned to her, unfastened his cloak and settled it over her own.

"I do not care for the ocean."

His brows went up. "Why? The shipwreck?"

"That too." She swallowed. "I lost... a friend to the sea."

"I am sorry for your loss. I too have lost men. To the sea and in battle. It never gets easier."

He wrapped an arm around her, offering her his warmth.

Her teeth chattered as she replayed that day.

"How do you go on? Not think about losing them all the time?"

Nicholas took his time before he answered.

"I wake and do what needs done. Those lost in battle died as they wished, fighting. The others? They would want me to continue, to remember them and not to succumb to sorrow."

He took her hand in his.

"In time, the pain dulls, but it never leaves us."

"That's what I was afraid of."

Jane hoped the woman who shared her name had not suffered as the sea took her.

Mistaking her trembling for fear, Nicholas tucked a lock of hair behind her ear.

"I will protect you. With my body and my life. If you do not care for the sea, you never need come to the water. The castle overlooks the channel so I can do nothing about the view other than bar the window."

"No, it's fine. I won't swim in the ocean ever again."

He nodded. "You almost perished. The sea would be hungry for you."

Before he lifted her up on the horse, Jane took a breath.

"I am feeling better but I find I cannot recall the date."

He stopped and turned to her. "'Tis the third of December."

"What year might it be?"

Nicholas lifted her up on the horse.

"'Tis the Year of Our Lord 1348."

She swayed, would have fallen if he hadn't held on to her.

"Of course. Traveling by ship I lost track of time."

He made a noise in the back of his throat as he turned the horse toward the castle.

Somehow, she had fallen almost seven hundred years through time, and not just to any time, but to a time of upheaval and plague. As if she hadn't been through enough of a pandemic over the past few years.

It was a lot to take in.

9

There was so much activity on a day-to-day basis at Winterborne that it reminded her of a movie in full production. Guess Jane shouldn't have been surprised that it took so many people to keep such a large home running smoothly. All the hustle and bustle made her miss being on set though she didn't miss all the yelling and drama, The week passed quickly as she settled into a routine.

For the first time since she'd started working for Josie, Jane found herself with plenty of free time.

She loved going to the stables to see the horses. While she wasn't by any means an accomplished rider, she'd gotten the basics down. The men still teased her about falling off the horse. It was only the one time, but she had a feeling they'd tease her about it for a long while to come.

Riding was more enjoyable than she'd thought it would be. The horses each had their own personality, the black one

Nicholas usually rode was likely to bite, while the ginger colored mare was sweet with people and had an attitude with the other horses, making Jane laugh. Riding and exploring the grounds was a good way to keep out of the way of people cooking and cleaning.

One skill Jane hadn't learned that would have been useful here? Cooking. Her mom was big on salads or cooking on the grill so Jane didn't know how to cook a chicken or make a pie though she had made bread at a class once. Her limited skill set comprised making spaghetti, pizza, and macaroni and cheese from the box with the packet of cheese sauce. Usually she made the mac and cheese when her mom was out so she didn't have to hear the lecture about processed food.

Thoughts of home made her throat close up, her stomach clench. Surely by now the studio had notified her mom that she was missing? Or did Josie think she'd quit and gone home without getting the water from Bath? If so, no one would know she'd been in an accident, there would be no reason to call her mom.

Startled by the thought of her mom not knowing she was missing, let alone the fates or some supernatural force had trapped her in medieval England, Jane reached out and pressed her palms against the cold stone until her heart stopped beating like she'd run five miles.

The first thing she usually did upon waking, well after availing herself of the cold garderobe, was to sit in the window seat and look out to see what was happening around the castle, to see what Nicholas was doing, and who was coming and going.

The medieval bathroom was a tiny closet-sized room with a stone bench. There were leaves and old rags in place of toilet paper. Dried herbs hung from an iron hook to help with the smell though with the ocean air it wasn't bad this high up. The padded seat was more comfortable than she thought it would be. There was a wooden lid over the seat, covering the opening, which helped keep cold air from blowing in, though when she lifted the lid to do her business, well, let's just say that blast of fresh air was rather like taking a cold shower.

Nicholas was calm, competent, and cared for his people. The guy was up with the sun going about his lordly duties, checking on the men, practicing swordplay in the lists, riding out to the woods, seeing to repairs on the buildings damaged in a previous fire, and making sure the larder was stocked for the coming winter.

The guy was never too busy to stop and show one of the boys running around a move with a sword, or to stop and help a little girl struggling to carry a basket of eggs to the kitchens.

There wasn't a sit down meal at breakfast, it was more of a grab yourself a chunk of bread, slice of cheese, and a cup of ale, and go about your business kind of meal. She'd never cared that much for beer but had gotten used to it filling her up in the morning.

Some mornings Maria brought her breakfast and other times she'd wander down to the kitchens and grab a bite on her way out to explore the castle and the grounds.

Whenever she left the castle proper, two of the knights went with her to guard her from whatever threat Nicholas seemed to think might lurk nearby. The first couple of times were awkward, but she'd gotten used to the men so it no longer bothered her and gave her time to practice her Norman French. They laughed at her pronunciation and how she messed up the words.

People she talked to during her wanderings said the winter was colder than usual this year. The few merchants the guards let into the castle, came bearing news of people not having enough food for winter since the summer had been so wet, much of the harvest had rotted in the fields. People who lived at Winterborne and on the lands were well fed and wouldn't starve, thanks to Nicholas.

No matter how much Jane bundled up she was always chilly, especially when the wind blew in from the ocean. She was grateful for the fur-lined cloak and the clothes the other Jane had brought with her. What were the odds that they were the same size? Almost the same size, as Jane was taller and not as big in the bust. The generously cut tunics were meant to be belted, so the bust area didn't matter. Her boots showed but from what she understood, as long as she didn't show her bare ankles or legs it was fine. The thought of people here seeing a modern-day California beach made Jane grin.

The other Jane packed long tunic dresses made of wool, which were itchy on their own, but fine with the soft linen chemises underneath. The hand embroidery decorating the garments was stunning. Every dress embellished with some kind of design, from fruits and vegetables to leaves and animals all around the hem and necklines.

Maybe later in the week she'd seek out a few of the women and see if they might teach her the basics of embroidery?

Other than the embroidered slippers, the other Jane's shoes must have gone down with the ship so Nicholas had shoes made for her from soft leather in a rich brown and another pair in black. When she'd asked why there were pockets in the boots, he'd looked at her oddly then laughed, telling her 'twas for a lady's dagger. He was shocked she didn't have daggers or carry a blade on her person at all times.

A young girl, who proudly informed Jane that she had turned nine years old this past summer, showed up every morning to help her dress, and every evening to help her get ready for bed.

Yesterday, she'd been delighted to see Jane had her bedding and meager things moved to the small alcove off Jane's bedroom. The kid had been sleeping in the kitchens, which while perfectly acceptable, wasn't to her. Maria was quiet in the morning, lighting the fire and fetching water without making a sound so Jane could sleep. On the plus side of being stuck here, she'd never slept more soundly, waking fully rested each day.

Maria was shy and quiet but was finally warming up to her. "Mistress?"

Startled, she turned from the window. Jane pulled the heavy glass closed, latching it so it wouldn't blow open and break. Her face was cold from the air blowing in as she'd been watching Nicholas in the lists.

Watching him with a sword was like watching a prima

ballerina in the prime of her career. The sword was an exten-
sion of his body as he moved. How strange that a sword could
be beautiful and deadly at the same time.

Every once in a while, he would turn and look up at her to
make sure she'd seen him disarm his opponent or when he'd
done something amazing, like a backflip. And if her heart
beat faster, it was only at the possibility of harm coming to
him, not at how he made her feel.

🐜 10 🐜

“**G**ood morning, Maria.”

The girl's brown hair hung in a braid halfway down her back, the end tied with a bit of blue ribbon.

“There was a strange man.”

The girl frowned.

“He was hiding behind a cart watching our lord.”

She shook her head, wrinkling her cute little nose.

“I did not care for the look of him. He looked like the other men but different. He is up to no good.”

People forgot Maria was around since she was small for her age, quiet, and moved without a sound. The kid would have made an excellent spy.

“Would you recognize him if you saw him again?”

“Oh, yes. He is wicked.”

Jane tossed the blanket on the bed, now knowing better

than to fold the blanket or make the bed herself. The maid had been so upset that Jane cleaned her own room and made the bed that she'd burst into tears, sure she'd be sacked for not properly caring for the soon-to-be mistress of Winterborne. So now, Jane happily let her normal state of messiness run rampant.

Maria thought it was odd that Jane requested a cup of saltwater every morning and evening which she used to rinse her mouth out. Surfers knew saltwater could help prevent tooth decay. After questioning Jane why she used water from the sea, Maria had also started rinsing her mouth out with saltwater even as she made a face, saying it was too salty, and making Jane laugh, banishing her worry for a while about how to get back home.

She helped Jane dress in a dark green tunic and chemise, tying her sleeves, then brushed and braided her hair as they sat in front of the fire.

"We shall look for this wicked man so we may tell Nicholas of him."

The child beamed, showing a missing tooth in the front.

When Jane opened the door, a teenage boy pushed off the wall.

"I am to watch over you whilst my lord is in the lists."

The dogs were there, tails wagging. Maria fussed over them, kissing the giant beasts on their heads and whispering in their ears.

The boy shifted from foot to foot.

"My lord says I must go where ye go."

A hopeful look filled his face.

"Might ye wish to go to the lists?"

"To watch Nicholas practice his swordplay?" Jane tapped a finger to her lips as if thinking. As the boy's face fell, she put him out of his misery.

"Of course I do. Lead the way."

He practically ran down the corridor, Maria on his heels, the dogs barking, tails wagging so hard, she could feel the wind on her face as she trailed after them.

Instead of going out the big front doors, the boy detoured to the kitchens.

"Why are we stopping? I thought you were eager to get to the lists?"

His scrawny shoulders slumped as if the weight of the world fell upon them. Teenage boys were, in her opinion, just as dramatic as teenage girls, only quieter about it.

"You must eat. My lord says so."

He handed her a cup.

A sniff told her it was beer.

"Ale? For the morning meal?" What would people think when she went back home and drank beer for breakfast?

He nodded, "Aye 'tis good for you."

"I'd prefer water."

The boy let out a sigh that sounded exactly like Nicholas when he was trying to explain the current politics of the time to her.

"Drink the ale, then you may have water."

Bossy kid.

He frowned at the bread and cheese, then with a shrug, handed her a thick slab of cheese and a hunk of brown bread.

Maria, mouth full, snuck a piece of bread to each dog. The dogs looked at her with adoring eyes.

"My apologies."

She finished the ale and took a bite of the dark brown bread.

"Apologies for what?"

"The white bread isn't ready. Brown bread is for us, not a lady as yourself."

Jane chewed. "It's delicious."

She finished the cheese and regarded him with a half smile as her mom's voice sounded in her head.

"White bread is prettier, but brown bread has more nutrients."

At his blank look, she elaborated.

"It's good for you, better than white bread."

He frowned at her. "My lord said you were odd."

When he scowled, he looked exactly like Nicholas. Somebody had an enormous case of hero worship. She could relate. It was as if someone had fed their preferences for the perfect book boyfriend into a computer and it generated Lord Winterborne.

They made their way out of the warm kitchens into the chilly day as Jane pulled her cloak tighter.

Talk about odd. She had the same name as the woman he was supposed to marry, a woman declared dead with the rest of the people on the ship. Her poor family. At least they would have closure, the knowledge of what happened to their daughter, unlike Jane's mom.

"Jane. Have ye come to watch me best this lot? To gaze

upon my manly form?"

Nicholas had tied his hair back with a black ribbon. He wore a worn black tunic and hose, a hole in the elbow and another in the knee, what she would have called knock around clothes, and her grandmother, before she passed, would have called rags.

"You are very manly." She put a finger to her lips. "I don't know if you can best them without messing up your pretty face. They look rather fearsome to me."

She teased him as the men jeered and made rude gestures to each other. A few of the curses made her brows fly up. They were the first things the men had taught her, saying it was amusing to hear such a pretty little thing curse like a knight.

Nicholas clapped a hand over his heart, eyes twinkling.

"The lady wounds me."

Then with a fierce grin, he pulled a second sword and nodded to the men. "By twos then."

Sir Cedric, a knight with thighs like tree trunks, called out a wager. The rest followed, and not wanting to be left out, Jane dug in the pouch at her waist, now glad she'd let Nicholas talk her into wearing it, then decided she had something better to wager.

"I wager a special dish called mac and cheese to be served to the winner on Christmas." She shouted to be heard over the men.

There was a beat of silence, then they all started hurling insults at each other, swearing they would win the wager and her special food. Nicholas winked at her.

"Come on then, lads. Who will best me?" He taunted.

Hopefully, she could recreate a medieval version of her favorite food. When she told the cooks how she remembered the dough was made and then dried, usually in the sun, though she thought it might be warm enough in the kitchens, they assured her it would be done. There was cheese and milk to melt to make the sauce, and she could boil the dried pasta in a pot over the fire. It might be awful but she was determined to give it a whirl.

As she watched him fight, a chill settled over her skin. While this demonstration was playacting, it was preparation for the real thing. Practice for war. Men would die. The thought of him dying made Jane clench her skirts, her heart beating faster. No, he couldn't die. He was so vibrant, so full of life, men like him had to live forever.

Maria came back from her adventure as she called it. Or as Jane called it, snooping, and stood before her, dogs by her side.

"The wicked man must be hiding. Will you help me look for him?"

The dog leaned against Jane's legs, the other dog sat next to Maria, who ruffled the ears of the wolfhound.

"They are almost done, then we will search."

There was the sound of steel against steel, a loud curse, and then Nicholas stood before her, sweating, a look of satisfaction on his face.

He called out so all the men could hear. "The mac and cheese shall be mine."

There were good-natured grumblings as the men took their leave.

When he sat next to her on the stone wall, he smelled of salt, leather, and horse.

"You were very good."

He nodded. "Aye, I was."

"Not modest either." She grinned then cocked her head. "Why do you always wear black?"

A knight passing by snorted. "Black hides the blood."

He said it so matter-of-factly that for a moment all she could do was blink.

"Jane?"

Nicholas pulled her close. He made a noise in the back of his throat.

"Do not worry overmuch for me, I will not die."

She leaned against his shoulder. "You better not. It would vex me."

A small chuckle escaped. "I should not wish to vex my lady."

He intertwined his fingers with hers.

"Would you care to—"

But before he could finish the question, a man came trotting over, needing him for something. He kissed her hand, making her blush, then left as she watched him go.

Maria shook her head. "The women in the kitchens say when a man looks at a lady like our lord looks at you there will be a wedding and then a babe."

She frowned. "Where does the babe come from?"

Nope. Not going there yet. Jane jumped up, the dogs did as well, ready for wherever they were going.

"Let's see if we can find where this awful man is hiding."

Distracted, Maria chattered on, forgetting about babies.

As she told Jane some long story about a bird and a rabbit, Jane still couldn't believe she was here.

When she was alone, she'd tried wishing to go home but nothing happened. The lake might have had something to do with her traveling through time but the lake was in her time. The sea was where they found her in the past, and as much as she wanted to go back to her own time, her fear of the water held her back.

She'd gone down to the cove, but her first step in the water made it hard to breathe. No matter how she tried, she couldn't go in the water. Shaking and spent, she gave up after the third try.

They searched the castle, the stables, and a few outbuildings with no luck. Ready to call it quits, a feeling told Jane something was wrong. Not knowing how she knew, she shoved Maria. The girl fell to the ground, crying, as Jane heard a whizzing noise followed by a sharp pain like her arm was on fire.

When she opened her eyes, Maria was standing over her, eyes huge, cheeks wet, an arrow in her hands.

"Someone tried to kill you, mistress." She scowled. "I know 'twas that damn wicked man."

The dog growled.

"Go." Jane pointed. Both dogs took off running.

Why was her arm so warm when the rest of her was shivering? When she touched the sleeve, feeling the tear, it came away red.

"I'm bleeding. Did you know that blood is warm?"

There were shouts, from faraway she heard his voice but couldn't answer. She hoped the dogs would bite a chunk out of whoever wished them harm. It was the last thought she had before everything went dark.

11

The shriek stopped Nicholas in the doorway of the garrison as men came running.

"'Tis the little one." Sir Cedric drew his blade.

A crowd gathered in the courtyard near the chicken coop. As he neared, they parted. Maria sat on the ground beside Jane, crying, an arrow in her arms. When she saw him, she jumped up, holding the arrow out, wetness streaming down her face.

"We... were... walking... it came out... of nowhere. My mistress saved me. She pushed me out of the way."

She gave him the arrow and threw her arms around him, sobbing until he thought his own heart would cleave in two.

"'Tis my fault she's dead." When she pulled away, she was scowling out over the courtyard.

"Mistress Jane set the dogs after the wicked man."

Before he could give the order, his men were off, following the tracks in the mud left by the dogs.

"Do not worry, child. Mistress Jane is strong. She will be well." With a deep breath, he prayed he was right as he lifted Jane, holding her close as blood dripped down her arm.

Her eyes fluttered open. "What happened?" She blinked at him, pale as a winter moon.

The woman who had taken him unawares, stolen his heart and soul, frowned.

"I've ruined my dress."

Nicholas carried her across the courtyard, bellowing for the healer.

"I will buy you a hundred dresses."

He took her to the kitchens, the warmest place in the castle, set her gently on a stool and cleared the table with the sweep of his arm, sending vegetables flying and crockery shattering against the stone floor.

He took off his cloak, laid it on the table, and then picked her up and gently laid her down. Frowning, he pulled off his tunic, balled it up and placed it under her head.

"If I'd known this was all it would take to get you to take your shirt off, I would have jumped in front of an arrow weeks ago."

Before he could stop it, a smile tugged the corner of his mouth up.

"You only need ask and I will gladly show off my manly form, though if maidens and crones faint who will do the work?"

A half laugh, half groan escaped. "Don't make me laugh,

it's like I can feel the blood dripping out of my arm when I do. So disgusting," she mumbled.

The healer arrived, barking out orders as Nicholas kept out of the way, knowing she would take care of the woman he loved, much as it pained him to let her go.

He was dozing in a chair by the fire when he felt a shift in the air. Nicholas jumped to his feet, daggers drawn.

"What happened?"

"Jane." Relief washed through him like the waves to the shore. He took her hand in his, reassuring himself she was well.

"You saved Maria. How did you know to push her out of the way? Did you see the man with the arrow?"

He helped her sit up. When she swayed, he gathered her in his arms and sat in the chair by the fire, settling her in his lap, wrapping his cloak around her.

"I don't know, I had a bad feeling."

He nodded. "Aye. A brush of the spirits telling us aught is amiss. I have had those feelings in battle, it has kept me from losing my head many a time."

She looked at the bandage, ran her finger around it. "I feel fine. Can we go for a walk?"

A chuckle escaped. "The healer gave you something for the pain along with a bit of brandy."

"No wonder I feel so good."

Her eyes were enormous, her cheeks pink, but when he touched her forehead she was not fevered, thank the gods.

"You were fortunate indeed, 'twas only a scratch."

She held his hand, running her fingers over the multitude of scars. "Who is trying to kill us and why?"

Nicholas frowned.

"I do not know."

He talked of the other accidents that had befallen him, how someone had shoved her in front of a wagon. Then he pressed his lips together, knowing it would not be long until they found this worthless cur.

"The men found a bit of blood. The dogs did well. They are searching the grounds, it will not be long until we will find this enemy."

THE NEXT DAY, HIS JANE DECLARED HERSELF BETTER AND asked him to take her riding. Promised him if they saw people she would stay away from them in case they were ill. When she had eaten bacon, bread, cheese, and finished a cup of ale, he declared her fit to ride. 'Twas important she kept her strength up.

They had not yet found the man, who had made use of the old tunnels and escaped through the labyrinth of caves by the cove. If the fates were smiling upon them, Nicholas hoped the man had drowned when the tide rose. His grand-mere had drowned a pirate thus, by chaining him to the rocks out in the cove's water so when the tide came in, the man drowned. 'Twas an awful way to die.

"Could we go to the last lake you told me about? Is it far?"

She wore a blue tunic today, leaving her hair loose. She was wearing the dark burgundy cloak embroidered with flowers he had made for her.

"Aye." He looked over at her, her hair loose and flowing, a smile upon her face as they rode.

"You told me you will not go in the sea, so why do you walk along the shore?"

She flinched. "The ocean reminds me of those I have lost."

They rode in companionable silence to the lake. The skies were silver, the scent of rain hung heavy in the air.

Nicholas lifted her off the horse.

"We cannot stay overlong, it will rain soon."

Her smile warmed him as the sun. "I don't need much time."

He let the horses graze while he watched her, wondering why she requested to visit the lakes? Was it some odd custom from whence she came?

What was she doing? 'Twas as if she were going to—

Jane tossed the cloak to the ground and jumped in the lake. She came up spluttering.

"Damnable wench." Nicholas did not know if he wanted to beat her or hold her close to take away the grief she felt at being so far from her kin.

Moments later, she screamed his name, clawing at the bank of the water.

He lifted her out, hauled her against him.

"Saints preserve me, woman. What the bloody hell were you thinking?"

"Nothing happened. I'm fine. Too many memories." She said, teeth chattering so hard he could hardly understand her.

He wrapped both cloaks around her, lifted her up and mounted the horse. Her horse would follow them back, eager for a meal.

"Have you lost your wits? You will freeze and catch a chill," Nicholas grumbled. "You are most fortunate 'tis not as cold today."

"I'm sorry." She twisted around to look at him, sorrow filling her eyes, making him feel like a dolt.

"Nay, love. 'Tis me who should apologize. You lost everyone on the ship, are in a strange land away from your family, and everything here must seem odd."

He took a breath. "If you wish it, say, and I will send you back to them."

"No." It came out so quickly, he knew she meant it.

Nicholas nodded. "No more jumping in lakes. 'Tis the third time you have done so. I should have known what you were about to do. Wretched woman."

She leaned against him, a smile in her voice when she said, almost singing.

"You really like me, you want me to stay, you think I'm pretty."

Hrumph. He pressed his lips together so he would not laugh.

When they arrived at Winterborne, Nicholas bellowed for a warm bath and sent her to the chamber whilst he saw to the horses.

A while later he had supper sent to his chamber. Bread, cheese, ham, and warm spiced wine.

He knocked on the door to what used to be his own chamber.

When she opened it, her cheeks were pink, her hair still wet.

"I had supper sent up. Will ye join me?"

She threw herself into his arms, as he held her tight.

"Thank you. For letting me go to the lake, letting me grieve in my own way." She tilted her head back to look up at him. "For being you."

"I am rather fetching."

She rolled her eyes. "Whatever. I'm starved."

Whatever? What was whatever?

His lady was odd. But she was his, and Nicholas loved her with a fierceness he never thought possible.

12

Jane spent a delightful evening with Nicholas in his solar. He was attentive, caring, and always put her first. After they finished eating, she sat in front of the fire, leaning against his legs as he brushed her hair until it was dry, and crackling with static.

Maria brushed her hair every day, but before that, no one had brushed her hair other than a hairdresser. Her mom believed children should be independent and encouraged Jane to do her own thing, which had resulted in an unfortunate bout with pink hair, the time she shaved it all off to support a classmate with cancer, and when she refused to cut it, letting it grow past her butt. When it got stuck in a fan, she gave in and cut it so it was midway down her back.

Thank goodness she'd lucked out and met him. It could have been so much worse, landing in medieval England. Many of the nobility in this time treated women like property, and many marriages were transactional, love rarely factored in, though Nicholas swore his parents made a love match and were happy together. Just think, if a peasant had found her? She'd seen the living conditions, and shuddered thinking about sleeping on a mud floor, rats crawling in the walls while a goat snored next to her.

She'd tried jumping in the water at all three lakes they visited, but nothing worked. Each time, panic set in, memories rolling over her like the waves of the Pacific Ocean. Would she ever get over her fears?

It was late when he walked her across the corridor to her chamber. Nicholas leaned against the doorway, light from the torches in the walls casting half his face in shadow.

"Shall we go for a ride on the morrow?"

Jane looked up at him. "I'd like that very much. Do you think we need to worry about the plague, I mean the pestilence?"

He thought for a moment.

"Nay, we are not letting strangers in the gates, and those that must enter we check for fever and black spots. If we take care, we may go. I know how much it pleases you to ride."

He leaned closer, tucking a lock of hair behind her ear, fingertips tracing her jaw. Unconsciously, Jane leaned in, close enough to see flecks of blue in his eyes.

There was a shout, then the dogs ran down the corridor, a chunk of meat in their mouth, a boy from the kitchen fast on their heels, cursing.

The moment passed. Jane went to bed, tossing and turning, thinking about him almost kissing her. It was absurd really, the thought that she'd had such rotten luck dating, she had to travel back in time to medieval England to find a guy. But boy, oh boy, what a guy.

THE NEXT DAY NICHOLAS WAS INSTRUCTING HER ON HOW to shoot an arrow at a target, when one of his men brought a stained scrap of paper, sealed with green wax.

"The messenger was coughing so we bade him stay outside the gates and did not approach. He left the letter, and we left him food and a coin as you said we must."

Absently, he nodded to the man, turning the letter over, frowning.

"What's wrong?"

Jane was glad for a break, her arms tired from holding and pulling back the arrow. She'd talked him into letting her wear a tunic and hose, pointing out that if she wore one of his tunics, it would be like wearing a dress since it came down past her knees. He finally threw up his hands and found her a pair of hose that belonged to the squire. He didn't know it yet, but she was going to wear hose every day, they were so much easier to move around in than a dress.

"The nearby estate, owned by the king. The tiles on the floor of the hall and in our chambers came from a kiln there. 'Tis near to Winterborne."

He looked up, eyes searching for the man who had left. The guardsman was halfway across the lists when Nicholas called out.

"The sickness has come close. Be most vigilant. All must stay outside the gates, no one allowed in. If after five days they are well, then they may enter. We will provide food and drink while they wait."

A few days later a merchant selling cloth was admitted after his quarantine outside the castle walls. He filled them in on the latest gossip. The king and other nobility had left London for their holdings in the countryside, hoping to escape the Great Pestilence as it was called.

Many were dying. Winter had slowed the progression, but they weren't in the clear. This plague would hang around for years. Why hadn't she paid attention to when it ended? But that was the problem with things that didn't affect you personally, you didn't always pay attention.

There was a shortage of workers, not just laborers but craftsmen and servants as well. The merchant, a young guy who looked to be nineteen or twenty, with bright red hair, told them how he had traveled through towns burying their dead in mass graves, that the smell was so bad, people refused to walk past the churchyard.

When the man left, Jane debated how to tell Nicholas the little she knew. It was smart to keep the potentially infected away. While she thought she remembered that the viral form of the plague was rare, it existed. While he attended to his duties, she made her way up to the battlements to sit and think.

Later that afternoon, another letter arrived, this one had changed hands many times before finding its way to Winterborne. The letter came through the pub in the village carried by a man in a wagon delivering costly spices.

Nicholas found her on the battlements, looking out over the lands. She had come to love this place, the people, and most of all, him.

His face was pale as he held the letter out to her.

"What's wrong?"

She took the letter, but couldn't read it, the handwriting so elaborate it took her a minute to realize it was in another language as well. When she shook her head, he took it from her, probably thinking she was too upset to read it.

"Monsieur Silva and the rest of your family perished from the plague."

He pulled her into his arms, stroking her hair.

"As you were an only child, all of his riches will come to you. A ship is already on the way, bearing jewels and gold."

Nicholas led her over to a bench set into the wall, sheltered from the wind.

That poor girl. Maybe it was better the other Jane had drowned before finding out she'd lost her entire family.

"Thank you for telling me."

She had to tell him something. Jane wanted to scream that she couldn't go through another pandemic. In her own time it had been awful, but this? It was going to get so much worse.

What could she say? In the end, she channeled Josie.

"A fortune teller told my father that a great plague was coming. He said it would last several years, spread across all the lands by next summer, killing almost half the people in every country."

He was watching her closely. "You believe such tellers of tales?"

It was the only way to share the information without revealing how she knew, though her knowledge was limited given her indifference to history.

"I do. He was highly regarded. I do not know why my family did not flee to the countryside where it was safer." She took a breath. "We need cats."

His brows went up. "Cats? Some say they are wicked creatures."

She shook her head.

"They will kill the rats."

Jane traced a scar on his forearm. When he'd taken his tunic off to use as a pillow for her, there had been so many scars crisscrossing his body, it made her ache for the pain he must have suffered.

"Rats have fleas. The fortune teller was sure the fleas caused the Great Pestilence."

A nearby guard grunted. "The priest says 'tis a curse from God for our sins."

Nicholas rolled his eyes. "Do not listen to him. The priests are dying as well, so I would think they are wrong."

The guard pursed his lips.

Before they could argue about sins and who was being punished for them, Jane continued as an old nursery rhyme went through her head. *Ring Around the Rosie.*

"It's not just rats. Other animals can get sick. They will talk of this plague throughout the ages."

She wracked her brain, trying to remember anything helpful.

"The rushes need to be changed, the floors kept clean so fleas don't get in them. Lavender, sage, and rosemary are good for keeping fleas away. We can make sachets for the bedding and to dust the animals."

What was the other herb?

"Oh. Pennyroyal."

The guard shook his head. "My sister is a midwife, she says the herb can kill cats. She likes the awful animals. Says it can cause a woman to lose a babe."

"Right. No pennyroyal."

Nicholas nodded more to himself than to her. He looked to the guard. "See 'tis done."

The man nodded and left.

"I know my family did not survive, but if this helps keep us safe, it does not hurt to try what the fortune teller said."

He took her hands in his. "'Tis good you told me. We will try. 'Tis my duty to keep the people of Winterborne safe."

When he stood, he offered her his hand.

"Come. I have something to show you."

He led her to an underground passage that led from the larder to the main well beneath the courtyard which supplied the castle with water besides the well above.

It grew colder as they walked. The floor was dirt, the walls stone, with water trickling down. The wind blew through the tunnel, making her grateful for the warm cloak.

"What's that door?" It was an old oak door, scarred, with heavy iron hinges.

He glanced at it. "'Twas sealed up last year. It leads down to the cove but the passageway floods halfway up during high tide. A servant drowned, so I had it closed off."

They continued through another passageway that brought them up at the corner of the great hall.

One of his guardsmen caught sight of Nicholas and came rushing over. He kissed her on the cheek before he left.

❦

WHILE NICHOLAS WAS OFF DOING LORDLY THINGS THE next day, Jane sat and watched how rushes were made. They gathered grasses from near the river, dried and then wove them, almost like straw floor mats. The floors were swept before they put the mats down, then sprinkled herbs over them. It smelled fresh throughout the hall.

The midday meal was the largest meal of the day. Jane was in the kitchens warming herself when she saw a platter of salmon go by.

"Is that for dinner?"

The servant looked scandalized. "Nay, lady. 'Tis not for nobility."

That was crazy. Salmon was for peasants? In her time it was expensive.

Tablecloths covered the tables, there were napkins for wiping one's hands instead of using the tablecloths or the sleeves of their clothing. Servers circulated with a ewer of water which they poured over each diner's hands so they could wash before eating. There was a pipe in the wall where they refilled the ewers.

She looked to Nicholas. "Where does the water come from?"

He glanced over to the pipe. "From a cistern on top of the roof."

After a hearty meal, they washed their hands again, then the servants would clean the floors and replace the mats. Nicholas grumbled at the cost of the herbs but said if it kept his people well, he would gladly part with the gold.

After dinner, he turned to her, a smile on his face.

"I have something to show you in the stables."

Curious to see what had him so excited, Jane followed him, running into Maria, who was so excited she was hopping from foot to foot.

It was warm in the stables, peaceful as the horses ate content in their stalls.

"My middle brother, Hugh, sent us a gift. He's a monk at the abbey. Once the pestilence passes, he will visit."

Nicholas nodded to the stall.

"I told him what you said about cats so he sent these wee beasties."

Maria squealed and sat in the straw, a huge grey tomcat with faint stripes, green eyes, and a chunk missing from one ear, curled up in her lap.

The child petted him, leaning down to whisper in his ear, while the enormous tomcat purred, accepting her attentions.

He was a beautiful animal, though it looked like he'd been

in a scrap or two. Jane scratched his ears as the purring grew louder.

"Hugh assured me the abbey cats are the best at catching vermin."

He went to the next stall and came back with a tiny yellow striped kitten.

"For you, little one." He held the kitten out to Maria.

She cuddled the kitten, a huge grin on her face. "I love him."

"'Tis a her."

Maria nodded as Jane held the tomcat. He was solid, heavy in her arms as he was content to be held like a baby, his eyes closed in kitty bliss.

"I shall name her Honey after my favorite treat."

Jane looked at the gray striped cat. "What shall we name him?"

Maria giggled.

"Rollo, because he looks like a big round ball."

The cat opened one green eye as Nicholas threw back his head, laughing.

"They both must earn their keep. Honey needs to learn how to catch vermin from Rollo. They will live together so she can learn."

He kneeled down next to Maria, a look of utter adoration on her little face as she watched the kitten play.

"You will see that they have a bit of milk and are well-cared for."

She picked up the kitten, rocking her in her arms. "Can they sleep with us?"

Maria slept in a small alcove off of Jane's chamber. Her parents had died of a fever and an aunt brought her to work at the castle.

He looked to Jane. She nodded, a smile on her face.

"I've always wanted a cat. My mom is allergic so I never had animals growing up."

Nicholas gave her a strange look but said nothing as she realized her mistake too late to take it back.

He patted the kitten. "Take them to the kitchens and see that they have a bit of milk."

Maria carried Honey, calling to Rollo, who jumped out of Jane's arms and trotted along after them, tail twitching as he surveyed his domain.

Jane hugged him. He was solid, warm, so much so, she kept her arms around him, not wanting to let go. The moment stretched, the sounds of the horses, the muffled noises of people going about their business, calmed her.

He touched her hair.

"You have the most beautiful hair. So many colors and so thick."

There were flecks of gold along with the blue in his green eyes. He inclined his head, the warmth between them like a small furnace. Jane tilted her face up, his lips a hairsbreadth away.

Someone cleared their throat.

"My lord." One of the garrison knights coughed. "Apologies, my lord, but there has been a mishap."

❧ 13 ❧

Nicholas turned, looking over his shoulder to see Jane leaning against the stable wall, staring at nothing, a smile on her face, fingers touching her lips. A smile crept across his own face. She wanted him to kiss her.

'Twas time to ask her to wed. He knew the contracts were done, but he wanted Jane to want to wed him, not because her sire demanded his daughter obey. Ever since he found her on the shore, he had been wooing her, knowing she was the one for him. No other would do.

Hugh was right, he looked forward to talking with Jane at the end of each day. There were times he would seek her out, just to see what she was doing. She had so many questions about how things worked, thoughtful ideas on how to make Winterborne more efficient.

In time, he hoped she would tell him the truth of who she

was, for he had known from the moment she spoke, she was not Jane Silva. How she came to be on the beach amidst the shipwreck, his true intended nowhere to be found, he did not know, but suspected she had switched places with the other Jane.

Mayhap she had fallen in love with a stable hand or cook and ran away? Women told their secrets in their own time, and as he was certain she meant no harm to him or to Winterborne, he let her keep her womanly secrets. What was of the utmost import was that she loved him as he loved her.

How long Jacob stood before him, waiting, Nicholas did not know, so lost in thoughts of whence his Jane hailed, he had a hand on his blade before he marked the man as one of his own.

"What is amiss?"

"We did not know until today. The priest has been away for a fortnight. Someone has been sleeping in the chapel. They broke all the windows, destroyed everything inside."

With a curse, Nicholas made his way to the chapel, marked the rags on the floor in the corner out of sight of the windows. The expensive broken glass and debris scattered across the stone floors.

He frowned. "He is using the caves. Take a dozen men and do not return until you find him."

Jacob nodded. "I will see it done, my lord."

JANE FOUND SHE ENJOYED EMBROIDERY, THE SOOTHING sound of the needle moving through the cloth, the ability to create such beauty. She liked to wrap up in her cloak and a blanket, sit on the stone wall out of the wind and watch Nicholas in the lists while she stitched. When it got too cold or he decided she looked like she was catching a chill, she would go inside and sit by the fire, or find the women and sit with them while working on Christmas gifts for him.

She touched her fingers to her lips. He'd almost kissed her yesterday, and she'd been disappointed when they were interrupted.

It was time to tell him the truth. When you love someone you don't keep big secrets.

Not paying attention, she pricked her finger. A drop of blood welled up, landed on the embroidery, making her swear.

The lady next to her gasped.

"Sorry. The men have been teaching me their favorite curses while I'm working on my archery skills."

The woman was from a neighboring estate, had been traveling and returned to find everyone dead. With nowhere to go, being unwilling to stay there, she asked Nicholas for sanctuary. So far, she hadn't warmed up to Jane, but tried to wrap herself around Nicholas every time he came near. It had gotten so bad that he would send one of the guardsmen to fetch her if she was in the lady's solar with the woman. If she hadn't been so sure how much he cared for her, Jane would have been jealous as the woman was beautiful and wealthy.

Falling in love with him had snuck up on her. She thought

he felt the same, knew he cared for her, but he hadn't yet said the words.

The words were important.

It would be the new year soon, a time for letting go of old things, like hot showers, central air and heat, microwaves, movies, modern appliances, cars, and ice whenever she wanted it. Though she wouldn't miss cellphones and being available at all hours of the day and night.

On the other hand, Jane knew with bone-deep certainty she would have never found a guy like Nicholas in her own time.

TIME PASSED, CHRISTMAS CREPT CLOSER, AND CLOSER AS Jane worked to finish her gifts. It was easy to lose track of the days when there weren't any clocks or anywhere she had to be.

She was up on the battlements thinking about her own time when he appeared.

"Maria is just as quiet as you, sneaking up on me. Did you teach her how to move without making a sound?"

"Does she?" He looked thoughtful. "A lass with such a skill might be useful."

He stood next to her, looking out over the lands.

"Why are you melancholy?"

"I missed Thanksgiving. It was always my favorite holiday after Christmas." The words came out without a thought. Well, it was as good an opening as ever.

He turned to her, seeming to know she had something to say to him.

"Might we warm our feet by the fire with a cup of wine?"

The man didn't miss a beat.

"You look chilled."

Once they were settled by the fire, sitting next to each other in the new chairs his mother sent, she took a breath.

"I am not Jane Silva. My name is Jane Randall. I'm from California, like I tried to tell you before."

He waited as if he had all the time in the world. The patient look on his face gave her the courage to tell him.

"California is in America. A country yet to be discovered."

She stared into the fire not wanting to look in his eyes in case he didn't believe her and she lost her nerve. Then again, why would he believe her? If their situations were reversed, she wouldn't believe him.

"Thanksgiving is a holiday, that's, well, what it's turned into now is a time for family to come together to eat turkey, stuffing, mashed potatoes, cranberry relish, and other yummy things like apple pie. Lots of people watch football after. My parents used to invite all their friends over, we'd have a huge potluck dinner in the backyard and stay up until dawn, then they'd all go surfing."

"A new country?" He pursed his lips. "I do not know cranberry and football or surfing."

Jane rubbed her eyes. "I'm not explaining this very well."

She turned to him, took his hand in hers and took a chance.

"I was born twenty-three years ago in the year 2000."

His brows went up.

"The day you found me, I was in England. Not this England but the future. The year was 2023."

Her hand shook.

"I'm not your Jane. I don't know what happened to her, but I let you believe I was because I didn't know what else to do."

"The future? So many years from now." He stood and paced back and forth in front of the fire.

"You traveled through time? How?"

She slumped in the chair. "That's the big question. I do not know."

He turned to her. "Tell me everything."

The fact he hadn't called for wood to burn her or thrown her out, gave her courage.

"I think we're going to need more wine."

Nicholas went to the door, threw it open and bellowed for wine. They were both quiet, lost in their own thoughts until the serving boy left.

He poured them both a cup, pulled his chair over so he was facing her and nodded.

"Begin at the beginning."

So she did, as they talked deep into the night. Jane told him about her time. About modern technology. The movie set, Josie, food, hot water, airplanes. And then about the accident and coming to in the ocean. She told him about her dad. How he died surfing and how she was afraid of the water now.

"'Tis a marvel."

Relief flooded through her. "Do you believe me?"

Nicholas ran a hand through his hair.

"There are many old stories about people going to live with the faeries. Mayhap they have simply traveled to another time." He drained the wine and sat staring into the fire.

When he turned to her, she couldn't decipher the look on his face.

"Would you go back?"

Despair filled her. "Do you want me to?"

"Nay." He lifted her up, settled her on his lap. "Your time sounds wondrous. I thought you might not wish to stay."

A choked sob escaped. "I was afraid you wouldn't want me."

"I would wade through every plague house in the country to keep you by my side."

Nicholas stroked her cheek.

"Will you stay?"

"I'd like that very much." Thoughts of her mom flitted through Jane as Nicholas bombarded her with questions.

By the time he was satisfied, she was hoarse and tired. The sounds of the castle stirring told her it must be close to dawn.

She looked out the window as he came to stand next to her.

"Jane?"

She turned to him.

"Swear you will never leave me."

"Never. I'll stay with you always."

He pulled her to him, crushing her to his chest. Jane had

wondered if when they finally kissed it would be polite and gentle.

It was not. It was the kiss of a warrior going off to battle. That kiss worked its way all the way to her toes. By the time he pulled away, Jane felt untethered from the earth, floating amongst the stars. That one kiss had blown away every other kiss before. It was a promise, a beginning.

A look of pure male satisfaction filled his face. If she'd had a mirror, Jane knew she would look like he had kissed her senseless.

14

Built on top of an old pagan fortress, Winterborne stood above the landscape, the view unobscured from all directions so no enemy could sneak up on them, except this time the enemy came from below.

Whilst searching for the man who wished them harm, Nicholas knocked over a barrel, revealing a long forgotten passageway. He could see his breath as he followed the path into the earth.

The torch sputtered but did not go out as he made his way deeper into the passage. There were no cobwebs here, a sign it had been recently used. The floor was dirt, packed down from hundreds of years of feet walking along the same path so he was unable to discern any footprints.

The scent of saltwater and fresh air filled his senses as he turned the corner, so intent on thinking upon all Jane told him, that for the first time in his score and five years,

Nicholas Montgomery, Lord of Winterborne was caught unaware.

The blow came from inside a crevice in the stone wall. He glimpsed brown eyes, swarthy skin, and then nothing.

When Nicholas regained his wits, he found himself chained to the old hanging post in the hidden part of the cove, the water to his waist.

Unless one of his men came to the cove, making their way around to the far side where there was a natural break, they would not see Nicholas staked to die like a common pirate. The bastard had taken his blades, even the small knives in his boots.

With the wind blowing, none would hear him yell so he waited, shivering in the cold water.

When the man who had plagued them so, appeared, Nicholas frowned, unable to recall where he had met the man and why he wished him dead.

"Who are you?"

The man waded in the water. The cove was calm here as the rocks provided a buffer from the waves.

The man shook, not with cold but rage.

"You murdered my Jane. That harlot, whoever she is, is not her. She has even stolen her name. We were in love. My Jane wished to marry me, but her father wanted your title and the power of your name."

He punched Nicholas in the stomach, making him wince, the breath whooshing out of him.

"I told her I would come for her, to see what sort of man she would chain herself to all for the sake of a title. For a month I waited and watched. You English think you are better than everyone else."

The man lifted his hands to the heavens, out of his head with anger and grief.

"I watched the storm take the ship. The sea was too strong. I could not swim out to save her."

His breath returned, Nicholas raised his voice to be heard over the wind. A storm was brewing.

"It was you. The arrow. The stones from the battlements. You burned down the outbuildings. You pushed Jane in front of the wagon. The wicked man skulking about the castle."

"Don't use my beloved's name for your woman."

The man laughed, sounding possessed by evil spirits.

"All this time, and you stupid English could not find me."

The man took a tattered piece of cloth from his waist, kissed it, and held it up for him to see.

"This was my Jane's. She made it for me for our wedding. 'Tis your fault she is dead."

"I would have broken the betrothal if she came to me, told me she loved another. No man wants a woman who thinks of another while with him."

The man hesitated for a moment, then shook his head reaching for the jeweled dagger at his waist, the one with the emerald in the hilt, his own blade. To die by his own blade was a grave insult.

The man's brown eyes filled with rage as he held the blade to his neck.

"I will take your Jane and bring her here so you can watch as I slit her throat."

With a grim look, the man tied the wedding cloth around his mouth so he could not call out for aid if the wind calmed.

Nicholas thrashed against the chains but could not free himself. His hands and feet chained tightly to the sturdy post. The post was fashioned so he could not slide the chains up the post to escape, and for the first time in his life, Nicholas was helpless.

He turned his head towards Winterborne, begging the fates for one last look at the woman he loved more than life itself. Even in death he would watch over her. The blade flashed, piercing his flesh, as the man laughed into the face of the storm.

JANE DROPPED THE NEEDLE, THE LEATHER GLOVE SLIDING off her lap to the floor.

"Did you hear that?"

Maria looked up from playing with the kitten.

"Nay, mistress." She cocked her head, listening.

"There. I swear I heard something."

"I don't hear anything." Maria backed away, making the sign of the cross. "'Tis a spirit come to tempt you to your death."

It was no ghost. It was her father's voice, telling her to hurry, and it was coming from the beach.

"Run and find Sir William. Tell him I need the men down on the beach," Jane called out to the girl as she ran, cloak flapping behind her.

She didn't know if the men had returned from searching the caves yet, but surely someone would be at the garrison. If not, Maria would get one of the men from the battlements or she'd find the men in the caves.

Hurry. Her dad's voice beckoned.

As Jane ran, the skies turned black as the rain turned to sleet, obscuring her vision. She tripped and went sprawling, spitting out a clump of grass, scraping her palms.

The wind was blowing so hard it almost lifted her off her feet, the waves high as she carefully made her way down the steep steps to the cove.

"Nicholas!"

She screamed his name, but the wind silenced her voice. When the lightning flashed, the cove turned to daylight, but he wasn't there.

Hands on her knees, sweating and panting, Jane closed her eyes.

"Please, tell me where he is."

She didn't know how she knew, only that Jane was certain Nicholas was in grave danger.

This time, instead of words it was as if her dad held her hand, pulling her across the cove. Then the brief warmth was gone.

The next time the lightning flashed, she caught movement. Creeping closer, she took a deep breath, stepping into the water, holding onto the rocks as she made her way around them to the hidden part of the cove. It was in the shape of a U, there were tide pools and the water was calm here.

Nicholas had tried to get her to go in, to work on her fears but when she tried, the panic returned.

Icy water rushed into her boots as she shook from cold and terror. There in the inlet was a man. She strained to see, waiting for the next flash of lightning, breathing shallowly through her mouth as the water tried to pull her out to sea.

There. Nicholas was chained to the drowning post. The wind muffled her strangled cry.

Where were his men? What was taking them so long?

At the next flash of light, she saw the glint of a blade. That man was going to kill Nicholas.

Frantically feeling around for something she could use, Jane picked up a stone, holding onto the rocks with one hand as she made her way around the bend, and just like that, the water calmed. The fluttering in her chest was like a bird trying to escape its cage. If she didn't do something, he would die.

Lifting the rock over her head, Jane knew she'd only get one chance. The man was yelling at Nicholas, something about killing his Jane.

It all made sense now. He must have been in love with the other Jane and didn't know about the shipwreck or blamed Nicholas.

When the lightning flashed, she brought the rock down hard. They both went down into the water.

Get the keys.

She heard the voice again. It sounded like her dad, always looking out for her even as he gave her the freedom to be herself.

Shaking, she spit out a mouthful of saltwater as she grabbed hold of the guy's shirt. Scrambling to hold on, she slipped, grabbed at him again, this time touching his belt, then the feel of cold iron.

Jane yanked as the guy came to, thrashing. The keys came loose. She elbowed him in the face and jerked away, letting the water pull him out to sea.

The water was up to Nicholas mouth, she could see in the flashes of lightning the look in his eyes. He knew he was going to die.

"No!" She screamed and swam out to him, kicking off her boots. The terror suddenly gave way. For the first time since her dad died, Jane could breathe easy as she swam. It was like the time her dad taught her how to float, holding her up, telling her to move as one with the waves, to respect, not fear the ocean.

When she reached Nicholas, he was desperately trying to lift his head above the water.

"Nicholas." She held the heavy ring of keys up. "Hold on."

There was a gag tied around his mouth but she couldn't take the time to get it off, chains first.

As hard as she tried, Jane wasn't tall enough to get a grip on the chains above his head. He was trying to tell her something. Wasting precious seconds, she yanked the gag down.

"I can't reach them." Frantic, she tried again.

"Jane. Hold on to me and lift yourself up."

She wrapped herself around him, put one bare foot on his hip and pushed up with all her strength, grasping the post.

As she worked the key in the lock, she could see the water was up to his eyes.

"Nicholas hold on. Don't leave me."

The lock came free. Jane ripped the chains loose, pain shooting through her hands as blood dripped down. She let go, fell into the water and went under, trying to push him up.

Then she used his body to pull herself down to his feet, holding her breath, feeling for the chains. The water was murky from the storm, making it hard to see.

There. She grabbed hold of the chains, took the key and by touch found the lock. Lungs straining, she unlocked them, pulling the chains away as her fingers burned where she'd ripped off several nails.

She surfaced as Nicholas sunk to the bottom of the sea.

"No!"

There was a splash, then William and three other men were there, helping her pull Nicholas to the surface.

They got him to shore, turned him onto his side and pounded him on the back.

"Please, come back to me."

He was so pale.

Jane screamed. There was an awful retching sound and Nicholas spit up water.

He was alive.

"I thought you were gone."

He blinked at her, sleet pelting them as the thunder and lightning finally subsided. In all her life, she'd heard of thunder sleet but had never experienced it, until today.

Nicholas retched again. The men helped him up, supporting his weight.

His captain let out a breath. "The bastard caved in the tunnel. Wee Maria heard us and brought help. We came as fast as we could."

Something dark on the sand made Jane frown. She touched the spot, her fingers coming away red.

"You're bleeding."

"Bastard stabbed me with my own blade," he rasped.

Before she could fuss or look at the wound, Nicholas pulled a blade from the man next to him, rolled up into a crouch and bared his teeth.

He held up a hand. "He is mine."

There, coming out of the water, blade in his teeth was the man Jane thought she'd killed.

The man pointed the blade, ready to throw it.

"That is not Jane Silva, she is an imposter. She killed my Jane. You only wanted her fortune. It went to her when her family died from the plague. She must die."

Nicholas threw the dagger. The man fell. And this time did not rise as the sea took him.

He staggered as he turned to face them.

"He was out of his head. This is my lady and I will defend her with my body, my very life."

The men nodded.

His captain and one of the garrison knights caught Nicholas as he went to his knees.

William winked at Jane.

"What about the dowry?"

Nicholas shrugged, then winced. "Payment for the damage he caused to Winterborne."

Jane let them help him, knowing she couldn't carry him. He looked over his shoulder at her.

"You should have seen her. So fierce. My Jane is a fine warrior."

He stumbled and almost went down. The men caught him, worried looks on their faces.

When she lifted his tunic, she bit her lip. The wound was deep, bleeding freely.

15

By how much Nicholas grumbled over the next few days, Jane knew he was feeling better. The man was a terrible patient, demanding full meals instead of soup, telling her he needed to be up and about. When it got to where she wanted to throw something and scream, Jane called in reinforcements.

William and Cedric stood next to the bed, arms crossed over their chests, scowls on their faces.

"I have things to see to." Nicholas grumbled.

The man healed fast, nevertheless, he'd been stabbed. It wasn't like a paper cut.

"Aye?" His captain arched a brown. "What things?"

Nicholas huffed out a breath, and before she could clap a hand over her mouth, a tiny laugh escaped.

He glared at her.

"What, pray tell 'tis so humorous? I am perfectly well. 'Tis time for me to leave this damned chamber."

She straightened to her full five foot six inches and glared right back.

"You'll have to do better than that."

She stomped over and poked him in the stomach, on the opposite side where he'd been stabbed.

"I'm used to Josie, you're a pussycat compared to her."

Cedric snorted then paled when Nicholas turned his most fierce scowl on him.

Jane simply rolled her eyes.

"I was laughing because you sound just like Rollo when you make that huffing noise."

She waved a hand at him.

"But it's just... you."

The strangled cough made her press her lips together. William was trying his best not to laugh, he knew what she was going to say.

"You will tell me now." Nicholas bellowed.

In response, she simply lifted her shoulders, tapping one foot against the stone floor.

Hrumph. "Fine. I'll stay abed until I am released from this torture."

He gave her the look she called his puppy look.

"Will ye tell me now?"

With a sigh, she threw her arms up. "It's no big deal. It's just that—"

"Tell him, lass." William doubled over laughing as Cedric looked confused.

"When Rollo gets mad he goes and smacks the other cats. Then he sits in the chamber looking out the window and refuses to come to me or Maria. He won't look at us until we have fussed over and petted him, and told him how handsome and ferocious he is, then and only then will he deign to look at us."

She came to sit beside him, taking his hand in hers.

"I think you and Rollo are a lot alike."

The chunky tomcat in question, who had taken to sleeping next to Nicholas while he was recuperating, cracked one green eye, huffed and jumped off the bed, stalking out of the chamber, tail held high.

There was silence, then Nicholas snorted.

"Aye. You are right, we are alike." He patted the bed. "Come and fuss over me, feed me your vile soups and potions, I shall not complain."

She turned to Cedric and William.

"Did you hear that? He swears to be good."

She leaned down and kissed his cheek. "I'll be back soon."

When his men came to see him she made herself scarce, giving them time to talk. If she hovered over him, Jane knew it reminded him he had been injured, and he thought it made him look weak in front of his men. It didn't, but whatever. Men. They were such big babies when they were sick.

THE NEXT DAY WAS CHRISTMAS EVE. JANE PROMISED Nicholas he could come down after dinner. She would have let him get up this morning but she wanted enough time to finish the decorations.

Everyone pitched in to transform the castle into something out of a fairytale.

The washerwoman told Jane it would snow today. When she asked how she knew, the woman said whenever her knee ached it always snowed. It would be a rare treat, they rarely got much snow.

The great hall smelled amazing. The scents from the wood burning in the enormous hearths, mixed with herbs sprinkled on the floors, and the greenery decorating the hall.

Back home, her parents never decorated for Christmas. They put lights on the avocado and citrus trees in the backyard but that was it. Jane never had a real Christmas tree.

They'd strung greenery, holly, ivy, and bay leaves across the mantles and around the doorways. While there wasn't an actual Christmas tree like in the movies, they'd laid greenery everywhere they could and fashioned a sort of shrub looking tree out of greenery for the high table.

It looked so pretty. Nicholas told her they would provide a meal to those beholden to Winterborne, usually a feast for all, but with the pestilence, they would send each family home with a meal comprising: ale, beef, bacon, a chicken, stew, cheese, and even candles to light their feast.

Everyone in the kitchens had been working to get the meals ready. Tomorrow was Christmas and marked the beginning of the 12 days of Christmas, when all the servants were given time off.

She was admiring the hall, when she heard the commotion. Nicholas made his way across the hall, stopping to accept good wishes for his recovery. He'd shaved, bathed, and dressed in a blue tunic and hose, embroidered with stags, leaves, and trees, instead of his usual black clothing.

He pulled her close, leaned down and kissed her soundly, to the cheers of people in the hall.

"Wow. You look amazing."

She held him a moment longer, so grateful he was hers.

"Seems my tyrant lady knows what 'tis best for me."

Jane arched a brow.

"You have got to be the only man in all of history to tell a woman she is right and knows what is best."

"Isn't that the truth." A woman said as she scurried by, arms laden with clean bedding.

He turned, looking over the hall as she waited to hear what he'd say.

"You saw to all this?"

Nicholas touched the red ribbon she'd woven around the greenery.

"'Tis lovely."

"I'm so glad you like it."

She took his arm as they walked through the hall out into the wintry day.

"I have a confession to make."

He stilled, looked down at her. "You are not going to tell me you are married to another... in your own time?"

"What?" She rolled her eyes. "Don't be ridiculous. There was no one."

Then she went up on her tiptoes and kissed his cheek, inhaling the clean outdoorsy scent of him.

"There's no one but you."

They walked together, talking. And as time passed, Jane swore it had turned colder.

"Once this pestilence is over, I will take you to meet my brothers and my parents." He guided Jane around a partially frozen puddle.

"I'd like that. Nicholas?"

"Aye?"

Jane clenched a handful of fabric in her fist.

"I know some of the men know I am not the same Jane, but what will you tell your parents? You can't exactly tell them where I'm really from."

She still couldn't believe that he believed her. It was difficult, but she was so different that he said 'twas the only sensible explanation.

"Nay, we will let everyone believe you are the other Jane. She is gone. Her family taken by the sickness. 'Tis for the best."

She nodded, glad to have it cleared up.

As they walked, he told her about his family, his brothers, and growing up. In turn, she shared memories with him of her dad, and her own time. And in talking with him found it didn't hurt as much as it had before.

Good memories were precious. There were so many things she'd never worried about missing, secure in the knowledge her parents would always be there. Now she'd tasted the bitter knowledge of loss, knew how much it was possible to miss them when they were gone. At that moment, Jane would have given anything to take back the hateful things she'd said that day when she told her dad he put surfing before her and she hated him for it. She would have gladly gone surfing with him, knowing it made him happy.

Nicholas taught her how important it was to live, not just to exist as she'd been doing, but to thrive. To find joy in the smallest moments, like watching the dogs splash in the water, or seeing children play, their belly laughter ringing out across the courtyard, or watching Rollo stretch in the sun, content just to be. There were the moments spent sitting in front of the fire, talking about their days. Watching him practice in the lists. Being grateful the plague had spared them thus far.

Something wet landed on her nose.

"Jane, look, 'tis snowing."

Nicholas was like a little kid watching the snow fall, while she stood there like a statue, blinking.

"It's so pretty." She turned around in a circle, watching the snowflakes tumble through the air, the delight on people's faces. It was the most perfect day. Nicholas was so much better than a book boyfriend. He was real.

They were up on the battlements, watching the snow cover the tops of the trees, when he turned to her.

"Come, you will catch a chill and then I shall be the one demanding you stay abed."

She looked at him, committing every feature to memory, so thankful she'd found him.

Nicholas brushed snow from her hair. The guard moved away from them as Nicholas went down on one knee.

He held out a heavy gold ring covered with sapphires and diamonds.

"I love you, Jane. Enchanted from the first moment I saw you. You are the first one I wish to tell when something happens. When I wake, my thoughts are of you. Before I sleep, my last thoughts are of you. I look forward to us sitting by the fire at night, telling each other about our days. I will love you until we are dust. Will you marry me?"

She wiped the tears from her eyes.

"Yes, yes, I'll marry you."

Arms around him, Jane knew she was where she belonged. She had tried to go back to her own time and couldn't, so she had accepted this time and place, and as time passed, had fallen in love with Nicholas.

"I love you too. To the moon and back."

16

The pounding on the chamber door startled Jane and Maria awake. Honey jumped sideways hissing, while Rollo rolled over with a yawn, snuggling deeper in the covers.

"Who is it?" Jane yawned, stretching.

Maria ran to the chamber door, hair sticking out from her braid. She was rubbing her eyes as she passed Jane, still half-asleep. Usually, she was up early. All the excitement of Christmas Eve had worn her out.

She opened the door and there stood Nicholas, looking disgustingly cheerful for it being so early in the morning.

"A Merry Christmas to you, ladies."

His excitement was infectious. "It snowed all night."

Maria jumped up and down, so excited she could hardly stand it.

"I want to play in the snow. Can we?"

She ran to her room, dressed in about five seconds flat and ran past Jane and Nicholas.

"Whoa, stop."

Jane put her hands on her hips, trying to look serious, and failing miserably.

"Don't you want your presents first?"

She clapped her little hands together, eyes shining. "Presents? For me?"

The hopeful look on her face made Jane wonder if she'd ever had a nice Christmas?

The fire had burned down, the floors icy cold as Jane wrapped her cloak around her. She went to Nicholas, going up on her toes to kiss him, his cheek scratchy against her lips. He smelled like snow, the bark of the trees, and wood smoke.

"I have presents for you." She squeezed his hand.

His eyes sparkled. "And I for you." He bent down to stoke the fire.

Before she could take a guess, a boy from the kitchens brought a tray laden with bacon, ham, bread and cheese, along with spiced cider.

Nicholas said he had to go fetch the presents. So while he was gone, Jane ran to the garderobe, came back and dressed, and yanked a brush through her hair. She opened the trunk at the foot of the bed, pulling out the gifts she'd been working on for weeks.

When he came back, arms laden with packages, she and Maria were in front of the fire, barely able to contain their excitement.

"Who wants to go first?" He set the gifts on the stone window seat.

"Maria. Otherwise I think she might burst from all the excitement." Jane said.

Eyes shining, Maria clapped her hands together.

Nicholas gave her a new green dress, a pair of shoes, and ribbons for her hair.

"They are so beautiful." She stroked the dress, tried on the shoes, and wound the ribbons around her fingers.

Maria tried to scowl at the kitten and failed. Honey meowed at her, nudging her hand until Nicholas nodded and Maria gave the kitten a bit of bacon.

"I will keep these safe so Honey does not shred them."

Honey was a mischievous kitten, and if left unattended, got into all kinds of trouble, like shredding hair ribbons and jumping out from under the bed to attack the ankles of whoever was walking by.

The kitten also had a love of water though after she'd fallen into the moat and had to be fished out, the fur ball was more careful.

After she put her gifts away, Maria came to stand before them, hands behind her back. She went first to Nicholas, holding out her hand.

"For me?"

She had embroidered a flower on the end of a black ribbon. "For your hair, so it doesn't get into your eyes when you are in battle."

He made a show of admiring the ribbon.

"'Tis beautiful work. I will not fight today, but 'tis so lovely I must wear it so all the knights are envious."

He tied his hair back with the ribbon, as Maria beamed, showing off another missing tooth.

She turned to Jane, holding out her other hand.

"Lord Winterborne procured the pillowcase, but I did all the embroidery all by myself."

Embroidered all around the opening of the linen pillowcase were images of Honey and Rollo chasing birds.

"It's the most beautiful pillowcase I've ever seen." Jane hugged Maria, glad she couldn't feel the little girl's ribs so easily anymore. "Thank you."

It was Jane's turn.

"Are you ready?"

Nicholas gave her a slight nod, just as excited to see Maria's reaction.

"Close your eyes."

Maria hopped from foot to foot, eyes closed as Jane took her by the hand, leading her into the alcove which served as the girl's room.

"You can open them now."

Her hands flew to her face as she ran to the small trunk. Until now, she'd had to hang her clothes on a hook on the wall. Now she had a trunk in which to keep her things, just like Jane. A boy in the stables liked to paint, and had painted Honey and Rollo playing in a field of flowers on two sides. On the other two sides, he'd painted the cats catching several rats. Jane thought the scenes were bit gruesome, but Nicholas assured her they were fine.

"Thank you, mistress. I have never had anything as fine as the chest." Maria hugged her, then went to Nicholas and hugged him.

With a laugh, Jane sent her on her way.

"Go, have fun. But watch out for Honey, she's never seen snow before."

Maria scooped Honey up in her arms and scampered out of the chamber, leaving them alone.

Nicholas poured them both a cup of spiced cider.

"I think Rollo ate the rest of the bacon while she was opening her gifts."

The big tomcat blinked at them beside the fire, washing his paws.

Jane narrowed her eyes. "He does look rather guilty."

She couldn't stand it any longer.

"Come, sit by the fire, and open your presents."

When he sat, she brought out the gifts. She handed him the pair of leather gloves she'd finished. Since the area she was working with was small, she'd kept it simple, embroidering leaves around the cuffs.

"Such fine work." He stroked the black leather. "You lined them with fur to keep me warm."

She nodded. "Do they fit?"

He slid them on, flexing his hands. "A perfect fit."

Next was a black wool, fur-lined cloak. One of the women helped her with the embroidery. Jane had managed the vines and leaves, but the other woman stitched the stag and falcons.

She traded one of her rings for the materials to make the gifts and to have the cloak and dagger made. The ring was her

grandmother's, a simple gold band inset with a ruby and emerald. The look on his face told her it was worth it.

"The work 'tis beautiful."

He stood and put the cloak on, admiring the embroidery
as he turned around. He leaned over, kissing her soundly,
leaving her breathless.

"I thank ye, Jane."

She grinned. "There's one more present. Stay right there
and close your eyes." As she went to the bed where she'd
hidden the gift, Jane looked over her shoulder.

"No peeking."

Hrumph.

Careful not to make any noise, she pulled the dagger from
under the covers. Just in case he was peeking, she held it
behind her back until she was standing in front of him.

"Hold out your hands."

She laid the dagger across his palms.

"You can look now."

The look on his face told her it was the perfect gift.

"William helped me. He looked over the dagger to make
sure the weight was right."

It had a sapphire in the hilt and vines carved down the blade.

He spun it on his palm, tested the weight and nodded.

"A most wondrous gift."

Even though the dowry that belonged to the other Jane
wasn't hers, Nicholas insisted she have her own money, much
like his own mother. While she could have used some of it to
pay for the Christmas gifts, she wanted to use her money, and

since her money was in the future, she'd traded one of her rings.

She looked down at her hands to see the two rings she had left of her grandmother's and the ring he had given her. The heavy gold band was a comforting weight on her finger, the sapphires and diamonds sparkling in the firelight.

"I find I cannot wait any longer. Sit and close your eyes, my lady."

She waited, excited to see what he'd chosen.

"Open your eyes."

He had a new cloak for her, blue and lined with fur. It too was heavily embroidered along the hem with flowers and birds.

She laughed. "We gave each other the same gift."

"Aye, 'tis a good gift."

Then he turned and hefted a bundle from the other chair. Eyes, twinkling he held up his gift.

"No way." Jane jumped up, taking the clothes from him, hugging them to her chest.

"My own tunics and hose?"

"Mayhap you will quit stealing my squire's hose." He grumbled. "But Jane?"

She looked up at him, already deciding she'd wear the blue tunic and hose today to play in the snow.

"When family visits or other nobles come calling, promise me you will wear dresses."

Jane threw her arms around him. "I promise. But I'm wearing the blue today so we can have a snowball fight."

At that, he grinned. "If you throw like you shoot arrows, I have naught to worry over."

She smacked him on the arm. "We'll see about that."

He'd given her not only the blue tunic and hose, but a set in black, and another in green.

"Two more gifts." When he went across the hall to his chamber to get the rest of her gifts, she quickly changed into the blue tunic and hose. It was so much easier to move around in the hose. They were basically leggings. She'd appreciate the freedom of movement when she was running around in the snow.

"You've already given me so much," she said, the words fading away as he presented her with her own dagger. They totally thought alike.

Hers had a diamond in the hilt with flowers running down the blade.

"You will keep it with you at all times."

"It's beautiful. Thank you."

Nicholas swept her up in his arms, making her laugh.

"I don't need any more gifts. I got exactly what I wanted for Christmas. You. You're my Christmas Knight."

He kissed her, a loud smacking sound filling the air, making her laugh at this playful side of him.

"Come, I saved the best gift for last."

"Better than these? What is it?" He had been so generous, she couldn't imagine what else he had for her, she had everything she ever wanted.

He carried her down the stairs and through the hall, wishing everyone a Merry Christmas. The servants were in a good mood as today marked the start of the 12 Days of Christmas, and vacation time for them. She told him how she'd worked day and night for Josie, the ridiculous demands her old boss had made. Jane hoped whoever was working for her now didn't have an ulcer.

As he carried her out of the castle, she wiggled in his arms, but he held her tight.

"The snow is so pretty, let me down."

"Nay. There will be plenty of time for you to throw snow at me later."

He carried her to the stables, only putting her down once they were inside. He led her to the far stall.

"He is yours."

Jane looked in to see the most beautiful black horse she'd ever laid eyes on. The horse came over to sniff her hair as she stroked him.

"He's beautiful. What's his name?"

He gave her a carrot for the horse who happily took if from her.

"He is yours to name."

Jane thought for a moment. "Midnight."

"Aye, 'tis a good name."

The Christmas feast would take place at dinner in the middle of the day. Nicholas had been talking about her mac and cheese, making Jane hope her favorite dish would live up to the hype. There was pudding, made from thick porridge, currants, and dried fruit along with nutmeg and cinnamon, thick fruit custards, and pastries.

In addition, there would be leek and onion soup, fish, venison, mince pies made of shredded meat, fruit and spices, and there would be little partridges, which she wasn't sure how she felt about, but Cedric assured her they tasted like chicken.

If that wasn't enough to eat, there would also be legs of beef and mutton, bread and cheese, and the big flourish... an actual boar's head with an apple in its mouth.

Jane had seen the head in the kitchen. Nicholas laughed when she told him no thank you, it was a bit too realistic for her. The presentation of the boar's head was the event of the meal, with costumed dancers, and a special song as they brought it to the table.

"I'm not eating the boar's head."

"The more for me." Nicholas patted his perfectly flat stomach. "Shall we make war with the snowballs?"

Jane ran as fast as she could out of the stables, the dogs at her heels barking, tails wagging. Cedric was on her side while William sided with Nicholas as everyone got in on the fun, hurling snowballs, making snow angels, and laughing. Much needed laughter to banish thoughts of plague and sickness.

Jane rounded the corner of the garrison to hide, when she slipped in the slush, and went down hard, scraping her knee.

Great. She'd torn a hole in the new hose, and she was bleeding.

The wind picked up, a strange sound almost like a car engine revving, filled the air.

Nicholas rounded the corner, arm cocked back, ready to blast her with a snowball when he stopped, a look of fear on his face. They were behind the garrison, out of sight of everyone as ozone filled the air, the scent of something burning clogged her throat, and her hair, having come loose from the bun, floated around her face.

"What's happening?"

She held up her gloved hands, only they didn't look right. She could see them and she could see her hands holding onto her pink backpack on the bus from Bath.

"Nicholas, I'm scared."

"Jane?"

His voice came from far away as the wind howled, and ice fell from the trees.

In the next instant, the cold was gone. The scent of oranges filled the air, making her mouth water. The sun warmed her as she tilted her face up, enjoying the heat.

The sound of her mom's voice came closer as Jane stared into the mist. As she stared, her mom, walked up the steps of their house in California, board in hand, back from surfing early that morning. Jane followed her mom as she went to the bedroom, a suitcase open on the bed. The trip to Bermuda, she'd decided to go, after all.

The smell of the ocean clung to her mom's hair as she passed by, so close, but when Jane reached out to touch her, something made her snatch her hand back. Somehow she knew, if she touched anything, she'd end up back in her own time.

Jane turned. Through the fog she could see Nicholas, yelling, but no sound penetrated the mist. He was frantic, trying to reach her, but unable to move.

It was then she knew. Time to decide. Stay here in the past with him or go back to her own time.

As Jane watched her mom, she saw her sitting outside at the table in the backyard, eating an orange, barefoot. Her mom was a survivor, in time she would be whole again. And maybe somehow she'd know Jane was happy.

Jane turned to look at Nicholas. Remembered him saving her from the shipwreck. How he always put her first. The times he'd brought her a blanket before she asked. How his hand felt in hers. Every time he looked at her as if she were the most precious thing in the entire world. The love in his eyes that made her toes curl.

The choice was hers.

With a last glance at her mom, tears spilling down her face, Jane turned away and reached out to her future.

To him.

The mist dissipated. Nicholas lunged for her, hauling her to him, shaking.

"What happened? You were here and yet you were not. I could not reach ye."

"I saw my mom." She wiped the tears from her face. "I could have gone back to my own time."

"You stayed."

Jane loved him with a passion that astonished her. He was hers and she'd never let him go, just as she'd promised.

"I stayed. Always."

THANK YOU SO MUCH FOR READING! I HOPE YOU ENJOYED Christmas Knight. Next up is, A Scot for all Time, a brand new series featuring charming, roguish Highlanders. I hope you love this new series.

IF YOU'D LIKE TO RECEIVE AN EMAIL ABOUT MY UPCOMING new releases, please join my mailing list. Visit my website, www.cluhrs.com

ABOUT THE AUTHOR

Cynthia Luhrs spends her time out on the deck, looking at the mountains and imagining what if. Her rescued tiger cats like to disrupt her writing by sitting on the keyboard and demanding to be let in and out hundreds of times a day. She is overly fond of sparkly flip flops, books, and tea.

She writes women's fiction in the Blueberry Hill series, contemporary romance in the Magnolia Beach series, medieval time travel in the Knights Through Time series, steamy paranormal romance in the Shadow Walkers series, and heart-pounding thrillers in the There Was A Little Girl trilogy.

Keep up with her on her website

facebook.com/cynthialuhrsauthor
instagram.com/cynthialuhrs
bookbub.com/authors/cynthia-luhrs
goodreads.com/cynthialuhrsauthor

Made in United States
North Haven, CT
07 January 2023

30740720R00098